A Kite of Strength

An Anthology Curated by

Anushka Jain

Inkfeathers Publishing
www.inkfeathers.com

A Kite of Strength
Edited & Compiled by Anushka Jain
Print Edition

First Published in India in 2023
Inkfeathers Publishing
New Delhi 110095

ISBN 9789390882786

www.inkfeathers.com

Featuring the writings of

Soumya Tewari, Monica Dedich, Garv Archana, Anju Gupta, Ritu Ambwani, Aditya Jhingan, Pranav Uberoi, Sandhita Agarwal, Manish M Nair, Shreya Chauhan, Vaishnavi Kulkarni, Kashish Lewis, Tanisha Sharma, Apoorva Ravi, Ishita Sharma, Ashley Sanchez, Michael Tucker, Siddhi Chouthai, Parleen Oberoi, Sree Yelamanchi, Samresh Mahapatra, Sayani Halder, Claire Casapao, Dr. Shritama Das, Shreya Halder, Neeraja Krishnaswami, Anushka Jain

Disclaimer

The anthology 'A Kite of Strength' is a collection of 37 poems and 9 stories written by 27 authors who belong to different parts of the world.

Unless otherwise indicated, all the names, characters, objects, businesses, places, events, incidents—whether physical/non-physical, real/unreal, tangible/ intangible in whatsoever description used in this book are either the product of the author's imagination or used in a fictitious manner. Any resemblance to actual persons, objects, entities, living or dead, or actual events is purely coincidental.

The poems and stories published in this book are solely owned by their respective authors and are in no way intended to hurt anyone's religious, political, spiritual, brand, personal or fanatic beliefs and/or faith, whatsoever. In case, any sort of plagiarism is detected in the contents within this anthology or in case of any complaints, grievances, or objections, neither the anthology editor nor the publisher is to be held responsible.

I would like to dedicate this book to my mother, Lalita Jain. She has been my guiding light through the most difficult days of my life. She has taught me to stay strong throughout vast corridors of darkness and blessed me with the qualities of warmth and kindness. Her message of sailing on through the various shades of life has given me the courage to curate this book along with the Inkfeathers team. She has taught me to stand firmly in the face of adversity.

Through this book, I wish to leave behind a ray of hope for my beloved readers in their complicated days and sincerely wish that they get all the strength they may need to overcome their troubles. I just want to tell you that just like our five fingers in each of our hands is different, so is each day. Some days will be your best, and some will fade into sorrow and darkness. But none of them is the end. They are just small beginnings for a bright future. So, don't fall apart because it didn't work. Stay put as something bigger awaits.

Contents

Meet the Editor

Anushka Jain is a biotechnology student. Standing sharp in her twenties, she is a happy-go-lucky and cheerful soul who loves to live in the moment. She loves to take a stroll with herself in the park and also get her funny bones tickled with the ones she loves. She is someone who believes strongly in unity and loves to meet and spend time with new people. Anushka has the soul of an explorer that finds comfort in the warmth of nature. She has tried to bring this feeling through the words put together in this book with her co-authors. She loves to spend her time with herself and remind that the world maybe difficult but if she is strong, she will get through.

You can know her more on Instagram. Find her as @nushijain and her thoughts on @penning_thoughts_.

Preface

It was a bright, blissful day at school. I returned home, tired after a very long day, only to know that my mother had to go for a check-up to a cancer specialist in the evening. I was very heart broken inside. It was this feeling that was telling me that she won't come back home happily at night. It somehow became the truth. She came home, bearing the news of surgery. She was diagnosed with breast cancer. The next few days turned to be very hard for me. While my mother was entering the operation theatre, she, too, knew in her heart that she was impaired in permanence. She would not lead a normal, jolly life again. But I tried to make things easy for her as much as I could. But it did not work.

After this first encounter, two years had passed, only to bring worse days for a golden soul like her.

She had not thought that all of it would hit her again. Only this time, it also took her liver down with her. She had a long, hard struggle, which you will hear about in the first story of this book. Few days after this ended, my family was awestruck at me for the fact that even though I faced such terrible days, they had not seen me shed even a single drop of a tear from my eyes.

When I was a 6-year-old girl, I had seen people cry on news channels after a certain incident. I tried not to pay attention to it.

But it did not get off my mind. Later that night, I asked my mother, 'Mummy, why are these people crying so hard? What happened to them?'

She said, '*Beta* (child), they lost their near and dear ones in the accident. They are unable to bear that pain.'

I further asked her, 'Have you also cried this way before? Will I also cry like this someday? They look so upset, Mummy.'

She taught me that gains and losses are a part of life. The moment one human gains, another one loses. So, in order to make me emotionally independent, she made me make a promise. She asked me to promise her that I would not cry if anything befell her and took her away. At that age, I thought that mothers were eternal, and nothing happened to them. So, I convinced myself that she might be kidding with me, and I said yes.

But when I saw her struggling, I was pulled upon to be strong for her. Even though I knew things were going to end soon, I was there like a pillar for her. This promise remained deep seated in my mind and made me strong. I heard my family say that I had a very strong spirit. This made me not cry even while facing the loss of my closest and most favourite person. They were not aware of this for a very long time and came to believe that something must have happened that might have inspired me.

This thought prevailed in my mind for a very long period of time. It taught me the use of words to find solace, i.e., through writing my heart out. My first piece was a dedication to her.

This made me realise that there might be so many people out there looking for this power in their hearts. People might be facing so many problems ever since the pandemic came in to stay. Thus, I came up with the idea of this book to remind them that they are not alone in this. They have us. Each author has poured their hearts out through their poetry and narrations that can awaken the powerhouse of you, the readers.

People have talked about how hope is one of the brightest stars of our life in all kinds of situations. It pulls us through the roughest of days. It reminds us that good is not over. It is here to stay.

As the editor of this book, I really hope that you, my solicit reader, take this message back with you, and I wish that our pieces help you sail through the storm. And if you ever need peace or comfort in your heart when you are having a bad day, I hope you know where to be.

With all my love and regards strung into words for you,

~Anushka Jain

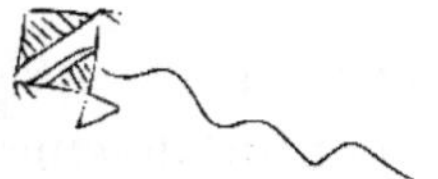

An Ode to God

Anushka Jain

It takes you nine months inside a woman's body to come out and experience life. The moment you walk out from there, your eyes meet a Goddess, your mother. She gives you her unconditional love, nourishment, and care. She keeps you strong and healthy.

You start caring for her the most. As a little toddler, you want her by your side when you walk to school. You grow up and learn to tell her everything that happened in school during the day. You make sure that she smiles when she is with you. You make sure to take care of her happiness in little things, like your first walk, first word, first dance step, and many other little moments.

Things become beautiful when you find your bond getting stronger with the most important woman in your life. You start paying attention to her, you take care of her. Your bond gets filled with endless love. Everything becomes serene. You want this to last forever and can't even imagine losing this one woman you love the most.

But things do turn bitter. The distance between life and death meeting and death prevailing is the most painful reality that you experience. I am sure, you can't even imagine yourself through this. But trust me, you always end up walking through this path of fire. It is a bitter aspect of life. Life throws everything at you at different junctures. Some of these are warm. Some turn bitter and cold.

The lockdown period introduced me to this and made me live this reality. One of my worst fears came true. I lost my mother. It was due to breast cancer.

Over the past five years, she had faced numerous hardships. Being a housewife, she was always on the family front. Striking the perfect balance was a difficult task, especially in a joint family. After my birth, she had almost forgotten her joys and started cherishing and living mine. I used to feel blessed to have her. I still feel that even though this bond of ours didn't last long, it was still the most beautiful chapter of my life that will remain etched deep in my heart forever.

So let me take you on one of the most heart-breaking journeys of my life. It was a rainy afternoon in Kolkata. The sanitiser van was passing and cleansing our locality of the COVID-19 virus. And it was the first time it had come there. So, we all were very excited as we had been enclosed in our houses for a long time and that became the most exciting feat to watch. While we were in the moment, I watched my mother walk to her room and lie down on the bed. She had recently completed her radiotherapy. So, I went up to her to see if she was alright. She had been complaining of uneasiness in her stomach. This went on for two days. On the third day, she had to be admitted to the hospital. That evening, my family was told that she just had a very short while left with her as she was tested positive for liver cancer. But I was unaware of this that night and slept by her side in the hospital. I was sitting next to her. She knew I was there though her senses started fading out. This made me realise that she was not doing well at all, and my family was hiding something about her from me. But I did not want to make the night any more difficult. So, I slept by her side once she had calmed down from her internal disturbances.

The next morning when I was home, I heard that her pulse and breathing rate were dropping frequently. I was becoming frantic.

Then, my grandparents told me that she was not going to get through this storm. This was the most devastating news I had ever received in my life. I rushed to see her with my father. We managed to have a little family time together and cherished some very happy moments that we spent together with tears in our eyes.

My father could not handle the situation for long, so he came back home to his parents' shelter. I was still there with my mother. A few moments after my father left, I received a call. I like to say that it was an angel's wish to see me bond warmly with my mother in our comfort zone for her last few moments. So, she told me that I should spend some warm exchanges of words with her frail hands in mine. I wanted to say a lot of things, shed a lot of tears and count upon a lot of joys with her. But I had very little time to do that. Hence, I decided to not waste even a single minute and started telling her about some funny things that my friends were talking to me about to help me cope with the situation. I told her about how our family was taking care of her. I narrated to her some stories from my college life that I had to tell her in person someday. I was assuring her that I would always take care of myself and surround myself with the people who care about me the most on my difficult and happy days alike.

Her breathing had normalised for the duration that I spent talking and sleeping next to her. Mumma felt good. I was right there, holding her hands and comforting her. I knew that she was hearing me and trying to send back to me a message of love and warmth from her end, even though she could not speak. It was this warm connection that we always felt for each other that made us know about each other best. And my heart never wanted the end of this soulful feeling.

The clock struck 7:30 p.m. I got a call from my brother saying he was here to pick me up and my uncle stepped into the room. I did not want to leave either of them there and just wanted to stay. I knew that the next time I would see her, would be on a white sheet.

But I had no broken feelings and emotions because I had told Mumma everything I felt back then to my heart's content. That night was the first night after 3 days that I had taken a proper meal. Losing her at that moment did not make me want to cry anymore. I slept well that night with my father's hand tightly held to me.

It was at 1:30 a.m. that she left. We got the news at 5:30 a.m. but I already knew in my heart. The only thing that amazed me was the courage I had in me to face the situation. I did not have even a single teardrop in my eyes. Not just did I take care of myself, I also was taking care of my family. I stood like a pillar for my father. I was acting more normal than anyone had expected. Some of the most unexpected people had become my source of strength and inner peace at the time. When I saw those faces, I realised that I did not need a breakdown to get through this. I just needed to keep my Mum in a sweet space in my memories and cherish them.

This thought changed me totally as a person. When I look back in time, I realised that my mother had brought me a long way from being the cranky school toddler to the emotionally strong woman I had carved out of myself with her help. I had never thought that I would experience this change and become so immensely mature.

My brain has been keeping me practical ever since Mumma went. But my heart still innocently longs for her every moment. But I have made my peace with this situation and learned to follow some of the life lessons she has given me. I have understood that every change begins in our hearts and sets in once we accept it. There are innumerable storms that we will face time and again. But we must remember that everything happens for a reason and every experience makes us stronger for the future.

Two difficult years have passed. But not one day goes by without me missing her and longing to tell her about the little joys and sorrows I walk through. Every minute I complete a task that I had been facing a lot of problems with, I want to run to her and tell her that I completed it. There are moments when I want to lie down on her lap and cry out loud. I want to listen to her sing "Chanda hai tu, mera suraj hai tu." I want to scream out in front of her and say everything. But she is no longer by my side. And I wish she were. I still do. But I like to believe that she is somewhere, looking out for me and sending her warmth and love.

I send out lots of love your way and I hope you will give your mom a tight hug at this small end of a beautiful story.

Life In a Poem

Anushka Jain

Set foot in this world
in your mother's arms,
Battle it to carve your niche
like your father has.
Think of a good time,
when your free will,
takes you to a world
when smiles were carefree.

Tread paths and pain equally,
Smile hard and celebrate endlessly.
Take yourself into a world,
where everyone is set free.

But don't let any arm
Rip yours apart
into the deep, dark shadow
of where they want you to be.

I. Me. Myself.

Anushka Jain

With mascara in her eyes,
and sharp red lips,
Flowers in her ears,
And shiny nail tips,
She walks in the dark,
Fierce like a lioness,
Bold like the queen,
with a shimmer in her dress.

The world is complex,
with souls that wander.
With their eyes and hearts,
over her skin, they ponder.
The beast is unleashed,
That is what they say,
when they watch her walk
and make her way.

But is it the dress,
Or is it the lipstick?
or the mascara?
or her walk?
Or her eyes that speak the truth?

It is the beast that you set free.
The ones that eye her
when she wants to be free.

But it is time.
to break them eyes free,
And rip apart the stereotype
of how a woman should be.
Instead, one should,
create a world that sets a tone,
of how all of us should be,
when a woman sets herself free.

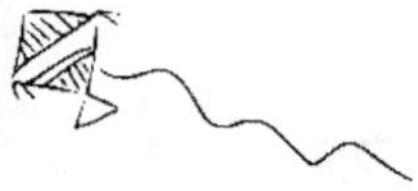

Love

Anushka Jain

Love.
A four-letter word,
enclosed by you and I.
But is it my crime?
is it why I should be tortured?
or you?
Does it make me less human,
or you more manly to not respect my love?
Does it change me?
Do I become a rag of the street?
Nope.
I choose to feel powerful.
I choose to stand with you.
I choose to be who I want to be.
So I guess I can choose to love you for who you are
and strengthen you,
And make sure you don't end this beautiful feeling
that nature has blessed us with.

Supporting the pride family!

Admissions

Anushka Jain

Jumps and leaps are not our things
Changes one too many.
From one city to another,
or one continent to another,
life always feels dizzy.
The rush of the hour,
Last-minute touches,
setting us apart.
building our roots for a bright tomorrow.
Submissions done
set in the anticipation.
A phase like none.
Hoping to get in.

What if you are left behind?
What if you don't?
Darkness ahead,
our future holds.
A thousand moments of self-doubt.
not one of relief.
Some letters rejoice
and some regret the same.

Things turn like a pendulum.
You don't know what time holds.
But whatever it is,
will always bring you magic,
one that takes you high
and teaches you to not look behind.
So kick your anticipation.
Stay fearless
Life is a rugged road,
ready to shape your soul.

When A Bird Learns How to Fly

Soumya Tewari

When a bird learns how to fly,
do you know how hard it tries?
One step, two step, three step, four,
five steps, sixth step, seven and more!
It falls back every time it thinks it can,
There's no procedure, not even a plan!
But still, it tries harder next time,
Just once again, it needs to cross that line
of stability and comfort found on the ground,
It flips its wings and takes another round,
to the places that once it was afraid to go.
Upwards, downwards, fast, and slow.
It keeps on trying until it's trained
to fly in the sky, right above those plains.
And slowly, it learns the trick so well.
Its flight seems like a wizard's magic spell.

When a bird learns how to fly,
do you know it has no one to trust when down it slides?
But still it tries, to fly once more,
because it's a long journey and there's so much to explore.
One step, two step, three it goes
up in the sky to all the places it knows,
Maybe it doesn't have the mentor it needs,
to fly with perfection,
to check its speed.
But when a bird learns how to fly,
it believes in itself by and by.
Ignoring all the steps that went wrong,
singing the tunes of its favourite song,
One step, two step, three step, four.
seems like it isn't afraid of anything anymore.

You Can~~not~~

Manish M. Nair

'You cannot be a manager here! It's not your cup of tea.' His senior manager shouted and fired him.

Nish heard a lot of cannot, everywhere he went.

'You cannot be a good life partner. It's pointless talking to you.'

'You cannot be a good friend. You're always away.'

'You cannot be a businessman. You don't have the right skills.'

At this point, he believed that he was incapable of even being a good person. The word "cannot" echoed everywhere he went. After a series of rejections, this was the first job he was able to get after completing his MBA.

Nish was a bit of an introvert and stuttered when he was amidst big crowds. Sometimes, he'd forget things as fast as a goldfish, but he loved quietly watching people and listening to their experiences. That is how he learned his way around life. He had big beautiful brown eyes and a heart that melted at the sound of a baby cooing or a puppy learning to bark. He was a talented young man, jovial and enthusiastic who carried hope and aspiration everywhere he went. The sky was the limit for his dreams, but fate and the cruelty of people never found a place for him. Most people took advantage of his soft, gentle nature while the rest deemed him to be 'less of a man' for being caring, lovable and understanding.

Nervousness had become his middle name after he lost his first job, yet he carried himself with respect and confidence in his pockets. He applied for another job. Then another, and another.

Everywhere he went, they'd ask why he left the previous company, and he would stutter and sweat. Tongue-tied, he'd just sit in the chair and look away. But he didn't stop. He began looking for jobs that could just pay him enough money to sustain his daily expenses—enough to have a roof on his head, food in his stomach and a blanket when he went to sleep. He had almost given up on the idea of finding a good job that an MBA graduate deserved. His endless efforts and days of jumping from one interview to another finally landed him at the door of a small company offering a long 12-hour desk job. They negotiated and out of desperation, he signed the contract for just the pay of Rs. 10,000 for a month.

Nish started his first day at work with enthusiasm and energy. He was early, neat and had done his homework about the people at the company. His training period was yet to begin, but he had already gathered enough intel from other employees and articles about the company's achievements. The previous night, his desk was filled with papers, highlighters, and files—researching. His efforts paid off on the first day when he managed to impress his trainer with his detailed knowledge.

Although his trainer and his experience in the training sessions were remarkable, he failed to connect with the senior managers. The dirty game of office politics seemed to follow him everywhere he went. Some of the teammates used their connections and contacts to get to the next levels in hardly a month while Nish was not able to get a promotion even after working amazingly well in the first few quarters.

He was from a modest family. Old parents with unfulfilled dreams were all that he had left in this world. He desired nothing but a place for himself in the world, where he could explore what he was and let his talents surprise him. What was his dream? He simply wanted to feel important, worthy, and valuable. He wanted to make his parents proud as he was his only support. It was just another ordinary day. No matter what his job was or how much pay, Nish walked as if he owned the world. Yet sometimes, it was remarkable how humble he was. Just as he was about to take a turn, he heard a voice, feeble and old.

'Take these chocolates for your kid, sir.' An old lady wearing hardly any warm clothes stretched out her hand. 'I haven't made any money today and my kids are hungry. Please, just take one.'

'Why do you sell these chocolates here?' Nish asked.

'I have nowhere else to go. My chocolates barely make enough for us to feed, sir.'

'Ah, such a cruel world!' Nish muttered. The old lady, despite her age, seemed to have sensitive ears.

'The world is not our enemy, sir. Hunger is. Sometimes I wish humans never had stomachs. There would be so much more peace.' Nish was in awe of this woman. She seemed wise.

'Besides, where will there be a place for a woman—especially a woman like me?'

He had nothing to say. It was all too overwhelming. He bought a handful of chocolates from her and continued walking, processing what he just encountered. That night, the clock seemed to be ticking faster than usual. He sat on his couch, staring at the chocolates. His mind was blank, empty, and wandering, until out of nowhere, something struck him. He pulled out his notebook and clicked his pen.

10 years later.

Murali Kumar and Jaya Kashyap sit at the table, with heads toward their TV. The 8 o'clock reporter spoke. 'Mompreneur ranks in the Top 10 non-profit organisations again this year. Founder Mr Nish

Kumar Kashyap to appear as chief guest at Mr President's red carpet tonight.'

'Could we please just turn off the news for the day?' Nish entered the room.

'But we love watching you on TV!' said Murali Kumar. 'It makes us feel…' Jaya held his hands, '...so proud of you, *baccha* (dear).'

There wasn't a big house or luxury cars parked but there was so much love and respect. Nish's definition of success was this. He had finally found his place in the world and his purpose in life. He was just where he wanted to be. 10 years ago, he had the courage to quit his job and created an idea that would change the lives of so many women around the world. He took smaller, less-paying part-time jobs to feed himself and his parents while he spent the rest of his time gathering women to build a community. Homemakers, homeless old mothers, beaten wives, abandoned girl children—all came together to cook and supply food for the needy at the lowest costs, sometimes even free. They slowly began raising funds from nearby communities to expand their reach. In a few years, Nish gave jobs to hundreds of women and fed thousands of hungry people.

'Please welcome the founder of Mompreneur.' The room roared in applause. That night, on that stage, when he went up to speak, the scene played in his head. 'You cannot be a leader.' The Senior Manager, who was now a CEO, was seated in the front row, applauding for him. 'Never let anyone tell you that you cannot. Because you can never know the unlimited power of the heart and how it can make people do wonders for the world,' he said as he left the stage.

The Mailbox

Samresh Mahapatra

I waited at the door,
from day one to,
the time infinity,
He used to come and go,
drop a mail up in the row,
I used to see him arrive,
before your father could derive,
about the brown chocolates,
and the pink notes,

I received the first letter,
The letter of the vigilant offer,
and the letter of the garland demise,
I heard it first that the riots had broken,
I heard first that the child got choked,
I was there, there then,
standing firm at the door!
Even then, even now!

I stand this day,
With your names engraved,
signifying the master,
who rolls his caster,
counting the last days,
where he lays,
On to the last day!
I did stand at the door
and see the fall of one,
and the rise of another.

I'd Stay

Samresh Mahapatra

All have I ever done in my life is run,
Run away from my problems,
Run away from commitments,
Run away from being accountable,
Run away from relationships,
Run away from failures,
Run away from people,
Run from pain,
Run away from the storms,
Run away from the rain.

But
For the first time, I have decided to stay,
Stay and see how the veils feel,
Stay and live each and every moment,
Stay and live each wind passing by,
Stay and wait to see a tomorrow,

Stay and wait till the clouds pass by,
Stay and wait for the sun to rise one day.

For the first time,
even he believed,
it is the Stay which actually lived,
not one more day,
but one more life.

My Mom, My Strength

Shreya Halder

You seem to be more didactic
over time,
You disseminate goodness
to all those around you,
You make everything feasible
even when it is not.
Flouting rules with you,
makes me feel alive.
When things feel insipid and humdrum,
like they lose their vigour and taste,
Your loquacious attitude changes everything.
You make me a little less misanthropic
a little less sad.
and make all the wrong feel right.
You, Mum, always make me better.

Battles of Time

Shreya Halder

A human I know,
a home I thought
to be my angel in disguise,
became my worst nightmare.

Trust is hard,
and finding your person harder,
But they made it seem easy at first,
and then broke me into small pieces next,

Everything I did,
every damn thing,
stood nowhere.

I won't let you be,
is all they said.
and kept making it work.

But little did they know,
that time was my antidote.

It helped me swing when no one did.
It made me strong to step ahead,
Lose myself
just to find me a better me.

Never had I thought
that a day will come,
When I will dream of a world
A heavenly one
that deprives me
of negatives like them
And allows me to sprint
far and wide

In this blessed ocean of loving thy self,
reminding to move on,
and not hold back.
or let them win.

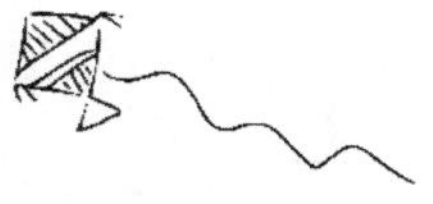

A Dying Conscience

Anju Gupta

An Indian with a wounded conscience

In the dead of the night
I meet my conscience
To see if it's still alive
As I think it's slowly fading
Day by day, night by night.

When I pay for a meal in a restaurant
an amount which might be a monthly income
of the guard who holds the door for me.
My conscience dies a little
And I can't find peace within.

When I buy a designer dress
which cost me a bomb
but I see women on the road
in tatters, trying to hide their pride.
My conscience dies a little
And I can't find peace within.

When I buy the vegetables from the vendor
and see his son "Chotu" at work
who should be in school studying like others,
but I try to look away
My conscience dies a little
And I can't find peace within.

When I shop for expensive gifts for my children
while returning, see the half-clad children
with an empty stomach and hungry eyes
selling toys at the red light.
My conscience dies a little
And I can't find peace within.

When my sick maid sends her daughter to work
bunking her school and completing my work
I should tell her to go back to school
but I look at the loaded sink with dishes
and let her work against my wishes.
My conscience dies a little
And I can't find peace within.

When my city is choking, and our lungs are clogging
I take my car to work every day
neither taking the metro nor arranging any car-pool
one car won't make any difference, I think.
My conscience dies a little
And I can't find peace within.

When I hear about a rape
or murder of a girl, I feel sadder
am thankful it wasn't my daughter
but I can't see myself in the mirror.
My conscience dies a bit
And I can't find peace within.

When people fight over caste, creed, and religion
my soul is wounded, and I feel helpless
my country is collapsing
but I blame the government and politicians
releasing myself of all accountabilities.
My conscience dies a little
And I can't find peace within.

When Covid spread its tentacles
people were wailing and dying
pleading for oxygen and hospital beds,
with my family, I was sitting in my cosy shell
feeling protected and not bothered about others.
My conscience dies a little
And I can't find peace within.

When in the dark, I visit my conscience
and find it still breathing, I am surprised
with my own hands, minute by minute
daily I kill it and conceal it
Still struggling to find peace within.

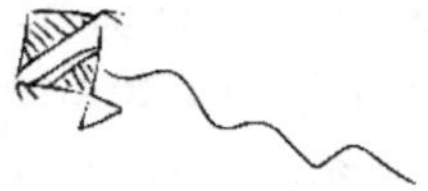

The Man.

Michael Tucker

An expanding horizon. Bright and unearthly. Imagine your vision filling up. A panorama of crustaceans and white horses. Froth, foam, a chalky jutting land-head of loam. The horizon still expands, drawing out further and further to encapsulate it all. The undulating buoy and the shimmering sands dilate your eye some more. Encapsulate it all. The washed-up weeds, the rotted flotsam and jetsam are thrown overboard by a lazy binman on some Yankee Warship miles and miles off. An obsolete lifebelt, drifting for thousands of kilometres from a capsized Danish cruiser, until it is deposited right here at your feet. The salty blood of Mother Earth or the World's natural sewer? Through which all garbage passes until it floats up to the surface damp and heavy… exposed to the light.

Zooming out, the man lifted his good eye from the camera's viewfinder. How his mind had started to wander since making his final decision last Sunday. It was now the Sunday after, in the inexhaustible succession of Sundays, and the weather had turned for the better. A sticky blue heat hovered over the tiny, beautiful cove for which the village was known. Postcards, paintings, even some tele-box advertisement had tapped into the blissful solitude of the beach where the man stood now. The man shook his head. A tele box advertisement. Ha! Not quite blissful solitude anymore, not when any family from Dagenham to Dundee could now see the bay's natural beauty, blinked into the privacy of their stuffy lounges at all hours! Heresy!

The thought made the man harrumph with tame disgust as he glinted back through the viewfinder, steadying his tripod into the sands underfoot. Sands which had not seemed so beautiful (nor as hot!) as the days from when the man had two functioning eyes. The world was changing from those golden days. Already had changed. The man had started to care less and less for the opinions of today. The ideas of the future only irritated him. The tradition was sick, convention wounded; he could see it all around. The man could only pray that they would survive.

The camera that the man glimpsed through really was state of the art. He bloody hoped so at least. It had cost him the vast majority of what he had left. He wanted the clearest photograph he could get. Various buttons and toggles decked out the bulky camera body which the man paid no heed to. Overcomplication. That was another insipid theme that had seeped into the modern age, he thought mildly to himself. Too much faff, too much tittle-tattle, just a bunch of hullabaloo. Verging on nonsensical. The man managed to find the whole image in focus at last; the soggy ankles of the beach in the foreground, the folds of salty seawater that bobbed the gleaming buoy far off in the distance.

SNAP.

The perfect picture.

Well, he supposed—*at least it is a damn good camera.* Maybe some new things were not so monstrous after all. The man paused for a moment as he waited for the photograph to emerge from the camera. He raised his filthy eyepatch and let the cool air flow against his oozing eye. The damn thing always itched. It had done for nigh on forty years, and the man had grown sick of it. The looks from the kids and wicked teenagers. The sniggers from the young harlots as they walked past in short skirts and knee-high socks, of course, did not stop the man from looking. His greasy old tongue flapped behind mucus-coated lips as he dared to imagine. Even still, this did not mean that he agreed with it—the unrestrained provocation of the body. The death of tradition. Again. Those bloody Eastern savages had it right, dressing their women up like walking carpets. His own Western women could simply not blame men for looking or touching anymore, not when they invited it on so willingly. Why, he may as well stroll through the High Street in his tightest briefs, sagging man-tits and forested thighs on display. That would make the young hussies squeak in disbelief! The man chortled out another cackle, spluttering as he did so, whacking his chest as you do to a failing car engine.

One of these racy little minxes he could remember staring at. Binoculars glued to his eyes as he gazed down the street from the safety of his one-bedroom town home, just watching her, filled with a mix of contempt and lust as she—

SNAP.

The man turned sharply. Eyes aflame with guilt at being caught halfway through his mental masturbation. The sound of stones crushed underfoot had emanated from up on the cliff path. Coming down was another man. A blurry, bowler-hatted figure took long strides as he descended the uncouth steps. Wonderful. Marvellous. Just blinkingly bloody excellent. One of the local riffraff, no doubt. Come to spoil his serenity. The man narrowed his eye accusingly as if the other man knew exactly what he was doing, coming down to the cove on a day like this. Ruining the man's last ever visit to his treasured beach. Well, at least he was not a dog walker, that much was a minor reli…

Just as these thoughts had formulated inside the man's fragile skull, the descending intruder had stopped, turned, called out, and then ushered forward some canine companion. The man's irritation boiled over as he took out his frustration with a firm stamp into the stony sand below. A stranger, he could just ignore, but a mutt you could not placate with a mere head nod. This would mean one thing only. Human interaction.

The dog would approach him, and he'd be obliged to pat it, before looking at the owner and moronically chattering, 'Who's a good doggy,' or 'He's got a lovely coat on him,' or some other hogwash. Well, that was it; he would have no time to sit and enjoy the salty breeze any longer. The man turned back to his camera as it whirled and buzzed. *Damn thing still has not produced anything yet. Come on, come on.* The harbinger and his hound would be here soon. The man looked into the camera slit—with his good eye of course—as if his peering into the inner workings would push out the photograph faster. Well, it was no use. The camera was constipated, and the wind suddenly felt very bitter on his pinched skin. He had to get off the beach.

Hesitating back towards the cliff steps, the man's worst fears had been confirmed. The trespasser and his Cerberus had reached the bottom, nonchalantly strolling in the man's general direction. This man could not have been more than forty years old, just a bloody youth, a thick moustache drooped over the lower portion of his face and a monocle adorned his left eye. What was most striking, however, was the unusual attire that this aloof customer sported. Full business wear. Pressed grey trousers, silver blazer, and waistcoat fastened over a plain white shirt, all tastefully flavoured with a red polka bow tie. The man could not help but gawk.

The gentleman and his dog sauntered along smoothly, seemingly unaware of the grimacing cyclops not twenty yards away. Now directly opposite each other, the strange man approvingly ruffled the space between his dog's ears and quietly turned, acknowledging the man's scowl with a slight tip of his bowler hat. The man almost broke character but managed to restrain an instinctive smile that nearly breached his lips, watching on in a mixture of scorn and wonder at this very odd, suited man.

He never once stepped out of rhythm, impervious to any looks of derision shot his way. The suited gent reached the far end of the cove; he delicately removed his hat, shoes, and grey blazer, unlaced his bow tie, and placed them neatly on a protruding rock. He crouched to a seat and slowly lowered his back to the sandy floor. Still as a corpse, the tide was not 2 metres from his toes. The dog sniffed away between some mossy rocks close to his master. He was untroubled. He was free. The man's stare had faded from disdain and was now showing something much closer to envy. *That's where I'm going, he thought. I need to leave.* Just like that, the man snapped back to consciousness. He had felt briefly lost in a dream watching this peculiar chap glide across his panorama. Suddenly, distracted by the silence, he looked down at the camera.

He saw his photograph which protruded from the slot. He plucked the image free and mulled it over. Perfect. It really was of the highest quality, thought the man; he marvelled at the sheer beauty of the landscape he had captured. It encapsulated it all. Bright and unearthly. He glanced warily one last time at the suited man. He still lay motionless. Satiated and unmoving. The man broke his look off, guilty at having watched so long. What was he thinking? Gaping at another gent like so? How crude of him! How, how very vulgar! With this thought, the man quickly packed up his camera and tripod, dusted off his jacket and hurried off. He paused and readied himself for the thoroughly exhausting climb back up the cliff stairs. Off he went, wheezing away as he made the sweaty ascent. Stopping frequently for shallow, sharp breaths, and hammering a bony old fist against his ribcage. He knew that his body was failing. Full of broken parts, creaky pistons, and shattered cogs. He was heading straight for the scrapyard. The sooner the bloody better!

The man took his final weary steps as he made it to the top of the cliff stairway. This infernal camera equipment had not made it any easier, crushing down his frail, raisin-like body as he marched from sea level to headland. The man turned back to see what distance he had come. A mere excuse to quickly shift his gaze to the now ant-like suited man one last time. Glaring down, the man felt the aching again. Creeping up through his brittle backbone. The sheer tranquillity this chap exuded! It was what he needed, what his breaking body craved! He envied it. He hated it!

Overwhelmed, he started away from the top of the steps with sudden determination. Removing his camera bag, the man paced across the plateau to the cliffside barrier. He went right up to the barrier and rested his camera bag atop it. With one firm push, he took out his frustration on the baggage, sending it over the side of the ridge and straight down to the rocks below. He did not need that technological junk anymore.

Pah! He spat down after it. Laughing with sheer liberation, adrenaline filled the man with what he had done. Feeling rebellious once more. Young even. Whooping and spluttering as the bag impacted the jagged stone and tumbled into the sea, he jigged on the spot. He took the picture out from his coat pocket and planted a mucus-stained kiss on the print with loving admiration. At least the overpriced pretentious tech had given him this one thing, something tangible, which gave him nothing but joy. An image that would stand still forever. That much he would be thankful for. But still, he detested what the camera stood for. Change. It stood for coloured televisions and gyrating hips, arrogant boys with quiffs. It was the end of an honest convention, which tied with tradition, which of course tied with morality. And morality tiptoed on the edge of a cheese wire, he was sick of waiting to see it falter.

But first, a drink, thought the man. He needed one last visit to The Hanged Man; this summer heat had given him a dry thirst for a whisky or two or three. Plus, he could use the extra courage. All he needed was a little nudge. Turning back from the barrier, the man started up the gravel which led around and left, to a small, tin-roofed public house. The place he had drowned his sorrows since he had been a young man, many moons ago now. The man wiped his sodden brow with his jacket sleeve as he approached the front door.

The Hanged Man was a converted fishing hut from way back in the day, long before the man was even born. The fisherman who had owned it all those years prior had a reputation as a fool and a drunkard. One night, when overflowing on homebrew, the fisherman had bragged about the strength of his new rod.

'That thing coold haul anythin'awt ah that bay,' he had boasted to his company. 'With 'is bran' new rod an' this sturdy line, ah coold even haul maself awt of that water.'

Well, of course, his company being blunt hooks themselves, the group decided to test the fisherman's theory along with his new rod. In a drunken stupor, roaring and heaving with laughter, they tied the line around the fisherman's waist and looped it through his prized rod, held firmly at the base by one of the parties. As the group watched on, their hilarity swiftly turned to horror. The fisherman leapt with drunken confidence from the hut's upper deck, the line slipped suddenly, up from his belly, contorted sickeningly around the fisherman's neck, and tore viciously through his gullet-like peach skin.

Hence the pub's ominous namesake. The Hanged Man. Or so the story went, anyway… at least it had been a strong rod. With a shudder, the man pushed open the thin wooden door which marked the entrance to the pub. Dim as a sea cave and just about as cold, it was certainly not a place for cosmopolitan folk. Just the way the man liked it. The landlord—who was the old landlord's grandson—stood there behind the bar; head cocked to the ceiling, denying any recognition of the man's entrance, only approaching as the man pulled a rickety barstool under his behind.

'Usual?' gruffed the old landlord's grandson, more of a statement than a question, as he uncorked the single malt and poured a double measure into a small glass. No ice. The man fumbled around in his pocket and smashed a hoard of coins into the new landlord's outstretched palm. The change returned and the man picked away at it, examining close with his good eye. Enough for one more. Hmph! He had important business to attend to! He took a long-drawn sip from the glass. Well, he supposed one more could do no harm; after all, he was in no hurry.

The whisky tasted sharp on the man's tongue, and hot as he gulped it down into his chest. He examined the old place methodically, some unruly litter squawked away in the corner, nattering about trivial tripe, no doubt. These little fools were the kind who would inherit the earth after he was gone. They cared nothing for the cliffs and the trees, knew nothing of politics and felt less than nothing for duty. The man lasered his eye at them as if to extract a tidbit of their childlike mutterings and prove his cynical judgement right. He only looked away when one of the rabbling rascals caught the man's stare and snickered back to his young wolfpack. Paranoia jolted up the man's spine as he quickly averted his gaze. The man lifted the tumbler to his lips. Whisky. His thoughts shifted, somehow trying to obscure his derisory thoughts. Some tedious guitar pop drifted out from the jukebox.

How many times he had been in here? He could not even begin to count, a place where he had cried with sorrow and cried with laughter, a place he had burst out with a song in moments of drunken euphoria. A place he had even scuffled with old rivals. Ha! Imagine trying to engage in a spot of the old fisticuffs now! No, he was tired of fighting. He wished for nothing more than a final drunken chant with former allies, to blow the tin roof of this unassuming watering hole one last time. He would even make do with the face of a former enemy breezing through that door. They would have a lot to talk about at least! The man shook his head and swigged down the remainder of his glass. He pushed the empty tumbler forwards on the bar and cleared his semi-quenched throat.

The new landlord stepped towards him. 'Another?' He took the man's silence as approval and once more uncorked the malt, pouring in a less than generous double. The man said nothing. He scrambled for the remainder of his change and jingled it into the oversized hands of the current landlord. The man sipped away. Out of money, out of time.

He was glad that the photograph had turned out the way he wanted; better, in fact. The unchanging rock. Himself, aligned forever with the shimmering bay. He sipped again. He felt emotions burning through his holey bones. An alcohol-induced rush shooting to his grey matter. Ah, starting to feel merry. He wanted to cry. Not tears of sadness and certainly not tears of joy. Tears for the evolving world he had once loved so much. Simple beauty that had been his to behold forever was now ending. Overrun by a new generation of materialistic youths and yobos. He missed his old world. When women were respectful and kids were silent, they just did as they were told. Men were real men, patriotic and strong. We got on with it, head bowed. Now it was all to be ruined. The new age. Well, he would not be sticking around to see it degenerate. His mind wandered back to the man on the beach, the man without a care. He remembered why he wanted to go beyond. For that feeling. Or lack of. Maybe, that chap and his dog could experience total serenity just lying on the sand. But he could not. Not anymore.

The man slugged down the last of his whisky in one sharp toss back of the head. He delicately placed his glass onto the bar before removing his keys, wallet, and eyepatch. He quietly arranged his possessions besides the glass, so not to alert the distracted grandson of the old landlord, who stood gormlessly, polishing glasses. Finally, the man removed the photograph he had taken from his inside pocket. Glancing over it with good and bad eyes, he flipped it over and took out his fountain pen. The man swished and flicked the inky tip across the back. 'Do not remember me.' The man placed it atop his glass. He softly stood up and motioned towards the door.

The landlord had still not paid him a glance, focused instead on the new colour TV which beamed in the corner of the room.

'I'm going to the sea,' called the man, 'that photograph, it encapsulates me; it captures it all.'

The man pulled his anorak back over his wiry shoulders and braced himself. He pushed through the door and emerged on the other side.

My Life, My Wants

Tanisha Sharma

You didn't judge me when I wore a burka.
You didn't judge me when I wore a saree and did all my chores
You never judged me when I used to put my wants...
my needs... aside and fulfilled yours…

So now,
You're not allowed to judge me when I wear a skirt,
You're not allowed to judge me when I come late from work,
Neither when I do parties nor when I do what I want,
Cause it's my effing life, and I'll live it as I want.

Courage and Strength

Vaishnavi Kulkarni

Courage is to face the problems.
Strength is to overcome it.

Courage is to just be yourself.
Strength is to motivate yourself.
Even when you hear others say discouraging things,
especially then,
Courage is to strengthen your freedom.
Many a times, we get the chance to do so but lose hope.

Courage is to take whatever comes
No matter what life throws
The strength is all in you
If you wish to seek it.

Sometimes,
The real difficulty is not in facing problems
But rather to embrace it and move on.
In fact, those tears are what make you stronger, not weaker.

When you think of it,
Not everyone has the chance to grow this way
To stand up to tough consequences in life.

But when it burdens you and pushes you
To a stage, you cannot take it anymore.
Taking a step back doesn't make you a loser.

Always remember—
The one who faces troubles,
Breaks through, adjust their sails to the wind
And learns from their failures and mistakes
Is the one who will achieve bigger things
And succeed in this little journey of life.

Breathe

Kashish Lewis

'Breathe,'
I say to myself every night
yet I struggle to find air
that can fill my lungs
but I know there will be
a tomorrow.

'Breathe,'
I say to myself every time I'm hurting
yet I struggle to calm down and stop crying
but I know that this moment shall pass.

'Breathe,'
I say to myself when I'm lost
yet I struggle to gather my thoughts
but I know that somewhere there is hope.

'Breathe,'
I say to myself when I feel empty
yet I struggle to sleep in peace
but I know that there is love.

'Breathe.
Breathe.
Breathe.'

I chant it like a mantra that has never left my lips
and I chant this even if I feel like I won't get through.

Because eventually, it gives me strength
and I live to fight another day with myself.

Becoming A Mother!

Dr Shritama Das

The loud noise of the toilet flush and the slamming of the door perfectly elaborated the sour mood of the young dentist, Dr Ruksat P. Mujammil. Mr Mujammil Sheikh was a marketer by profession and a very good husband. That morning after the banging of the door, when Mujammil walked in to check on his wife, Ruksat, with a dejected voice, she said to her husband, 'We failed again.' Mujammil said nothing and held her in his arms and they both sat on the bathroom floor for a while till Ruksat was mentally ready to start the day.

It had been a year since they were trying for a child. Doctors, medicines, temples, dargahs—they had done it all, but nothing seemed to have worked for them so far. To add to this was the family pressure. The constant nagging, 'You are 32 already, Ruksat! You are getting old! Have a child before it's too late,' pumping in guilt, frustration, and despair. Mujammil, however, was not affected much, and he preferred avoiding unnecessary arguments. Whenever such conversations would gear up and the initiator would be his mother, he would kiss her cheeks briefly and change the topic for the moment.

However, as days paced against the calendar at a hare's speed, so did the angst in Ruksat. Now, to increase up the sore in her heart, her husband contracted typhoid fever and was kept in isolation. She was torn between her husband and herself. But they say when all doors close, opens a new gateway. At least it was true for Ruksat and Mujammil. She missed her periods for the first time and also saw a double line on the strip. Finally! She was excited, wanted to break the news in a celestial way to Mujammil, but how could she? He was there lying on a corner of the bed, infuriated with a high fever. She tapped on his burning forehead with her cold fingers, 'Hey sleepyhead! Good morning. Our time for romance ends today. We're Pregnant!' She wanted to jump and hug and kiss and swirl and tease him, but all she did was, tucked the quilt around him tightly.

She dreamt of a "babymoon" during her first trimester. She had shortlisted places where they could go for their vacation. She was just waiting for the date scan with her baby for a green signal! But destiny had some other plans. She was forbidden to even travel on autorickshaws, leave aside a long journey. She had multiple medical conditions like PCOD, fibroids, adenomyosis, hypertension, and hypothyroidism to deal with along with her pregnancy. On the other hand, changing hormones instigated extreme nausea and morning sickness. Every time she would try eating anything, she would end up throwing up.

As the days passed by, her flat-toned waist and tummy bloated and sized up while her hopes and desires soared down. She tried everything in her power to keep herself busy and happy. But the pregnancy and house arrest made her very anxious. Her poetry, her books, her garden dried up eventually. She wasn't sick, but she was very lonely with her baby. The distances between Mujammil and her had suddenly shown up like rain without clouds. He was too careful when it came to her health. But was that enough? She had so many things in her silly mind. She was scared, happy, worried, lonely, and moody. There was no one with whom she could share her mind. She didn't want to go to her parents as they wouldn't understand her needs and make her fall into a strict routine. She didn't want that. Rather, Ruksat preferred to sit on her small balcony and watch the sun come up and down from dawn to dusk.

Now that her second trimester had started, Ruksat felt a bit more comfortable with her new body. She would now read stories, sing songs, and talk endlessly to her unborn baby. That day, when she went crazy for orange juice at midnight, the astonishing thing that calmed her nerves was a tiny grumble inside her tummy. She mistook it for a peristaltic sound. Oh! She was a doctor, you know. But then, it happened again. She felt like a tiny mouse had got inside her tummy and was trying to escape. Maybe, that was the first time when for a second the dormant mother in her soul had awakened. She sat up and calmly called upon her baby, 'Pudding, my dear baby, I know that is you. Yes, we call you Pudding. Do you like the name? Yes! You do! Are you sleepless tonight? Mommy will sing you a song. *Rock-a-bye baby on the treetop...'* the calm nights were filled with many such lullabies from now on.

The day when the radiologist showed them the newly formed limbs of the baby and the beating heart on the black and white monitor, all Ruksat could do was say a silent prayer, thanking the Almighty. The days seemed to be brighter now. The garden and the poetries once again came back to life. The sunsets were never lonely now for Ruksat. She had her little baby listening to her songs and her musings.

Amid everything, a grey cloud decided to shade their lives. The third-trimester scan revealed a slow growth in the baby's abdomen. Though it wasn't a grave concern medically, it did take a toll on Ruksat! She hardly slept, and always googled everything she could about her condition. Nothing seemed to satiate her racing mind. Now that the D-day was approaching, the young couple was at their wit's end. Ruksat either ate or sat with her eyes glued to the laptop while her hand traced her smooth round firm belly. But she couldn't sleep anymore. Her body was huge and heavy. She could barely walk.

It was just a week before her due date when they went into the clinic to get the scheduled check-up. That's when it happened. The doctor seemed so happy and was gazing merrily at the monitor while spreading the cold jelly on Ruksat's belly.

'What's the matter, Doctor?' The husky-voiced husband interrupted the doctor's mood.

'Oh! Ruksat and Mr Mujammil. You will smile like me, too, when you see this.' She pointed at the screen. 'Your little pumpkin is happy to meet you. He is smiling. This is a rare event. Rarely do you get to see an unborn baby smiling during a scan. You both are lucky.' Perhaps the delicateness of the moment had engulfed the "to-be-parents"; hence, neither of the two uttered a single word except to stare constantly at the little moving image on the screen.

It was the night when the media buzzed with the glorious return of the Indian Army Officer from the captivation of the enemies followed by a war-like situation on the borders. The excitement had perhaps infiltrated Ruksat and her baby. Baby Pudding was so excited that it started to show its kicking and dancing moves causing mini mountains on the belly.

The next day, Ruksat woke up from a dream, all panting and sweating. She looked at the ticking wall clock. It was 5:54 a.m. She realised the bed sheet was wet and she was confused if it was her water break or something else. She woke her husband, and they both now decided to rush to the hospital as by now the water was gushing out from Ruksat's body. Everyone was in panic mode. But not her. She was surprisingly calm and happy. Finally, the day had come when she would meet the beautiful baby and experience this superpower of mothers. Amid all these, still, she was too naïve and innocent. The graveness of childbirth didn't quite strike her mind. She accepted it as a blessing.

Ruksat by God's grace had a normal delivery like she always wanted. But it wasn't easy. She had a long 13 hours of labour, with her and the baby's blood pressure oscillating like a pendulum. The doctor warned her that if any further delay she would have to undergo emergency surgery. She also had to undergo some repair processes due to a tear. It seemed like forever in those times. It felt like she would give up at any moment. She almost bit on the iron railings of the bed with the increasing contractions. When the doctor asked her to push as the time had come, she couldn't help but ask a silly question, 'How do I do that?'

'It's a boy!' This statement didn't excite Ruksat as much as the first cry of her child. Her pain of getting stitched just vanished when she saw her little man. There he was; the perfect man. The perfect human. She needed nothing more; nothing else mattered anymore. She didn't quite realise the tears that welled up in her eyes when she saw her baby for the first time. He was a tiny little furball with bright shiny eyes, staring at Ruksat as if trying to recognise his mommy. When they took him outside for the father and other relatives to enjoy a glimpse, it felt like forever to Ruksat. She wanted to hold him in her arms. She wanted to cuddle him to her bosom and stop the time forever. She was a mother now! She knew she could be a mother to her child forever and in every birth. Everything else suddenly became distant, and there formed a small bubble, a bubble where lived Ruksat and her Pudding. She looked at his tiny, fragile fingers wrapped around her index finger while he tightly shut close his pink little eyes and was sleeping. She didn't know how to hold him, but she wanted to make him feel safe like he felt inside her.

The elated relatives had a lot to say and celebrate because Ruksat had delivered a boy. But she had nothing else to say or prove or do. The only thing she pledged to do was not to build an empire out of expectations from her baby. She knew she was nothing like her own mother when it came to parenting. She also knew she was going to have a hard time getting the hang of the whole situation, but she was happy. She couldn't stop smiling anymore. She felt complete now. The feeling of attachment and responsibility had become embedded in her heart. She felt like she was reborn in the same body. Despite all the sleepless nights, aching and shapeless body, everything seemed just perfect to Ruksat.

She was a mother now. That was all she knew!

Acceptance

Ritu Ambwani

Why is Maggi with ketchup not fine, but okay with sushi and wine?
Why is inter-caste marriage seen as a sin, but a marriage with heavy dowry calls for champagne?

Why is watching F. R. I. E. N. D. S. so cringey,
and not knowing about G. O. T. damage?

Why doesn't an artist's work get respect,
while a 9-5 job steals the show?

Why do queer, transgenders, or gays get glances of people's eyes,
while a girl and a boy can easily do anything just with the lies?

Why are college dropouts seen as a failure,
while Elon Musk and Bill Gates enjoy the status of billionaires?

Why does settling down mean marriage and kids,
and not a successful career and house with a Rolls Royce?

Why is the truth not accepted wrapped in sarcasm in comedies,
but movies with a bit of patriotism achieve glory?

Why are love letters and long walks underrated,
but Netflix and chill are sedated?

Why are cigarettes after sex necessary,
and holding hands seem imaginary?

Why is a person judged for their choices?
Why can't one just rejoice?

Why is one not accepted with flaws?
Why not just applause?

Move Ahead

Ishita Sharma

Think who you are and move ahead.
Think about what you want and move ahead.

No one will understand you,
No one will take you right,
People will condemn your modern thinking, but no worries
If you are right in your eyes, move ahead.

Many people will discourage you, but move ahead,
Many people will underestimate you, but move ahead,
Don't pay attention to people's jeers; just move ahead and move ahead.

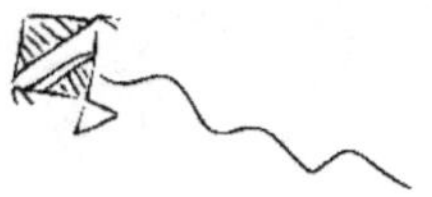

The Night Sky

Ishita Sharma

A dark sky with the stars and moon fills my heart
with a lot of fondness.

The night sky gives us a lesson that a single moon
can light the world,
But many stars together cannot as they are not capable of a lot.

The night sky is the idol of calmness.
The stars are the idol of absolute thoughts.

The night sky including the stars and moon gives us the
motivation to do more and more and to be happy lifelong.

Value of Life

Ishita Sharma

Life is not only about happiness.
Life is also about struggle and fights.
Life is what you make it.
Life is what you fight for.

Every sunrise inspires us to be a better version of ourselves.
Every sunset inspires us to cast our evil.

You think 'You can't win' but you can
If you think 'You can't be defeated ' then you are overconfident.

Take a step up against the wrong.
Raise your voice against any evil.
You can be what you want to be
You can change what you want to change.

Move ahead to your goals without thinking about jeering.
Move ahead in your life without thinking about what people think.

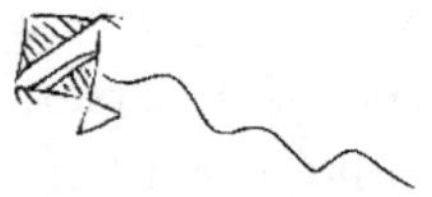

A Bird in a Cage

Aditya Jhingan

The clock struck 6 in the morning with the sun beginning to peep through the clouds. The rays of the sun brightened the backyard and the room. Arpita was up early to hear the chirping of the birds and get a beautiful view of the sunrise before starting her day.

She was fascinated by the view of the rays, seeing how perfectly they could brighten everything around her—the trees, flowers, fruits, and the skies full of dark clouds. After entering the kitchen, she flipped the lights on and started to prepare a cup of black coffee. Setting aflame the pan half-filled with water, adding a teaspoon of coffee to the mug, she poured the boiling water into the mug.

'The smell of freshly brewed coffee is heaven in the morning,' sighed Arpita.

Arpita Vyas was a final year college student, pursuing History Honours from her hometown, Delhi. From a reputed college, Delhi College of Arts and Commerce, Arpita was 22 years old with dark brown eyes and black, short hair. Due to her family being stubborn and old fashioned, nosy, and irrational, she was bound by her family's rules. That is why her wardrobe was mostly filled with full-sleeved T-shirts and pairs of jeans. She had to ask for her mother's permission for purchasing any type of dress or accessories, because she knew what her answer would be. 'Arpita, Dad would not like this dress because he thinks all of this is meaningless and a waste of money.' That is why she stopped asking anything she wanted.

Even after all this, her attitude towards others was very pleasant and heart-warming. She was an introverted type of a person. Despite being the only, helpful, and ambitious child, her artistic mind would capture every moment; every scene would be observed by her and recorded in her mind. Later, she would sketch or write about it in her diary. She also had her cold side, where if you tried to provoke her, she could act mean and smash you with her observable skills and hit you with your failures.

Arpita had a small group of college friends, but she wanted to achieve more out of her life. She wanted to spread her wings in the open air and fly like a bird. The only agenda of her life was to be like a bird who could travel around the globe and visit every place just to get a glimpse of beauty and life.

'Arpita!' shouted Mrs Sujata Vyas, her mom, 'Why are all the lights on? Shut them off. It's daytime, not night.' Her peace just got destroyed and she caught her coffee mug from falling.

'Maa! We do need light in the kitchen. It is as dark here as in Batman's cave,' said Arpita.

'Also, I only switched on one light in the kitchen, not like Papa. Every time, he would turn all the lights on, even the ones in the drawing-room. Anyway, what's for breakfast?'

'Get a bath first. Sit down while having anything, Arpita, and take a table mat, or you are going to spill the coffee everywhere. Gosh! You are a grown up now. Please learn some manners.'

'Maa...'

'No Maa, nothing! Go, get a shower, and get ready for college or you are going to be late.'

As Arpita was walking back to her room, a male voice called out, 'Arpita! Where are your manners? Are you not going to wish your dad before going to college?' It was Mr Sudheer Vyas, her dad.

Mr Sudheer Vyas was a government bank employee. Bald with a moustache, he was a very hard-working, sincere, and trustworthy employee, and even at his young age, he had been a very bright student. He used to be a sportsperson in his school and college days as well. A basketball player, even at the age of 48, he was very athletic and a very religious, old-fashioned, law-abiding, over-protective, and strict type of person.

'Good morning, Papa. Sorry, I didn't notice you there. Papa, can I go with my friend today to college if that is alright? Aren't you also getting late?' said Arpita in a very polite and hasty manner, as if she just wanted to get it off her chest.

Mr Vyas asked for a cup of coffee from his wife while pointing a finger towards the clock hanging on Arpita's head.

'It is already getting late, so why don't you get ready and head out with your friend? What is her name, again? You didn't tell me.'

Arpita stammered and said, 'Ri-Riya is her name, Papa, and she lives nearby only. May I go now?'

'Go, but be careful, and come straight home after your class,' he replied.

Arpita freshened up quickly and changed into her college clothes—a full-sleeved black T-shirt and a pair of dark blue jeans. While heading out, she grabbed an apple and waved goodbye to her parents.

Just as she was heading out, she heard Riya calling out to her and panting.

'Arpita! Arpita! Wait, wait…'

'Pump your brakes and take a deep breath first, Riya. What's wrong? Why are you running like a maniac? Was a dog chasing you?' asked Arpita.

'No, no. I wanted to catch up with you and go to college early since I would be staying late after college hours for preparation.'

'Wait, what preparation? Am I forgetting something, Riya?'

'Oh, Arpita! You are so good at studying, but I don't know what happens when it comes to partying and having fun. Don't you remember today is the annual function hosted by our seniors at college, and later on, it is followed by a massive party at night? Now, I don't care about any annual function, but the party is going to be wonderful since it is themed by Ajay.'

Arpita said, 'I barely remember that, Riya, and I can't come. You know that Maa and Papa won't allow me for that party. We have annual exams coming up as well. Shouldn't we worry about that?'

'Listen, Arpita, you have got to come. It's the annual party. Okay, look; I'll talk to your family and somehow, we'll manage to get you at the party, or we can probably lie.' Riya giggled.

'Lie! But Riya, what if Papa finds out…'

'No, first let me try. Also, tell me. Have you completed your Sociology assignment?'

'Assignment? Which assignment—Riya! Arpita!' interrupted Sameer, 'Both of you are coming to Ajay's party, right?'

'You mean to say the party themed by Ajay, right, Sameer?' asked Arpita.

'Yes. Riya, are you done with your Sociology assignment, and may I borrow your file? I haven't even started it. I'm sort of stuck on how we are supposed to conduct the interview and ask questions to our elders about the norms of society. They would obviously kick me out.'

'Do you honestly think Riya would do all that hard work all by herself? She is always busy with her social media and followers on Instagram.' Arpita giggled.

'Arpita, dear, now I'm confused. Are you trying to insult me or appreciate me? It's hard to tell while you are being smart. And besides that, you can call it whatever you want. I see this as being popular in today's world. People like seeing me on social media. I have at least ten thousand followers on Instagram.'

Arpita handed out her assignment file to Sameer. 'Here, you can take mine, but don't copy all the solutions. Also, try not to mess with it by flying it across the room like you always do with your best pal Ajay.'

'Sure. Tha...thanks, Arpita.'

'Sameer, I mean it. Don't, please?' said Arpita with her suspenseful eyes, staring at Sameer.

'Yeah, yeah. I have it safely. Thanks. I'll return it tomorrow. Now, let's meet each other after class, okay?'

'Sorry, guys. I'm not sure about today's party. I can't promise you if Papa will let me come or not, so meet you after class before heading back home.'

'It's okay, Arpita. You don't have to apologise,' said Sameer, 'and don't frown. Next time we will try to have a conversation with Mr Vyas, the basketball champion.' Sameer giggled.

Just then, the class bell rang.

'Sameer, stop it, *yaar* (friend). It is her dad. Okay, guys, meet you after class!' Riya walked away while waving to her friends. So did Sameer, but Arpita kept standing there and a sudden wave of emotions hit her.

She started thinking about why her Papa never let her do anything even after she did exactly what they wanted her to. Arpita started walking towards her class and sat down quietly in the last row so no one could disturb her.

Arpita's class got over early because Mrs Gupta, the substitution teacher, was sleeping after giving them homework.

She walked out, waiting for her friends, juggling a pen between her fingers; sometimes, she would drop it.

'Hi, Arpita! Where have you been?' asked Ajay.

Ajay Mittal was now a final year student, 25 years old. He flunked in History, Economics, and Mathematics. A below-average student. One could say his basic interest was mostly in partying and watching movies rather than studying. Ajay was medium built (neither too fat nor too thin but just about an average looking fellow). He had great smooth and silky black hair, dark brown eyes, and a very fair complexion. A little chubby cheek, though. His father was in the marketing field and a computer engineer.

'Arpita, are you coming to the party?' asked Mona and Ajay together.

'You must come. Ajay is making all the arrangements. It is his second time. Right, Ajay?' Mona pointed towards Ajay.

'Did you guys rehearse this last night? 'Cause you both are really bad performers,' Arpita giggled. 'Honestly, I can't promise you both, but I will try.' Deep down, Arpita knew Papa would not allow this.

Sameer interrupted, 'Let her be. She won't come. Mr Vyas, the so-called champion, won't let her.'

'Come on, Sameer. Stop teasing her like that. It is not her fault that her dad won't let her join a small party or enjoy just for a couple of hours,' Mona replied.

'Ajay, rather than partying or spending time with your friends all the time, why don't you study or even try to pay attention to any of the classes? Are you not interested in studying or did something really happen?'

Ajay, while avoiding her question, turned towards Mona and asked, 'What are the timings of the musical group you booked for the occasion?'

Arpita, in her mind, was rattling the same question again. *How can I crack the mystery of his life? He keeps on running without showing any signs of stopping. He is like a puzzle; I know he is in pain just like I am, and he is struggling as well. I still remember the day I saw his forearm filled with deep cuts. I wish he would let me in.*

The honk of her father's new Activa scooty put Arpita on alert and her expression made her look like she was caught by the police while robbing a bank.

Arpita turned around and said, 'Bye, guys! It is Papa's scooty. I should be going. See you tomorrow.' Riya shouted, 'Wait! Arpita!' But she was gone in a jiff.

While Arpita was riding with her dad on his scooty, she began with a normal conversation.

'Afternoon, Papa. How was work today? How is Mr Mukherjee doing? I heard from Maa that he was not well. Is he okay now? And how is –'

'Enough, Arpita! Can't you see? I'm driving! We'll talk later.' Her face drowned in sorrow and nervousness again.

A couple of houses away from their residence, Mr Vyas pumped the brakes of his scooty and said, 'Get down,' handing Arpita a 500-rupee note. 'Come home bringing a few bags of chips and a large pack of juice from the nearby store. We have guests.' He started the scooty and went straight home.

Arpita, while staring at the road, wiped her tears and continued walking towards the store. Her mind was a puzzle at that time. She started to beat herself up again. 'Why is my life like this? Why can't I do whatever I want to? My day began so beautifully and… I'm just tired of everything.' She sat down on the stairs of the store, began to cry, and started to wrestle over things in her head rather than facing her problems practically. She hoped that her dad would for once let her do whatever she wanted without asking for his permission. When she reached the entrance of her house, she heard a lot of laughter.

Arpita sighed. 'Guests are always like that. They drop by unknowingly and disturb the entire house decorum.'

While entering her house, she witnessed Mrs Rekha Sharma sitting on the couch like a giant, trying to destroy the beautiful couch while the springs made noises. Mrs Rekha Sharma was Arpita's aunt and Mr Vyas's sister.

'Arpita! Look at you. You have grown up into such a beautiful woman, my darling. Come here. Sit with me for a while. I want to talk to you. Tell me. Are you dating or not? At this age, you should be aware of young boys, Arpu. May I call you Arpu? I used to call you Arpu when you were 4.'

Arpita's temper was going through the roof. She never liked it if someone shouted in her ear, and why was she hugging her so tightly? The stench of her sweat was killing her. This was worse than Papa's anger.

'I'm good. How are you, *Bua* (aunt)?' asked Arpita while taking deep breaths. 'Thank you for all those compliments, and yes, Bua, you can call me by any name. Excuse me, I'll just go and wash my hands really quick. Papa, I have to ask you something. There is a party after 5 if you could allow–'

'You have finals coming over, Arpita. Stop all of this. Bua is here for a few days. You should go and start studying.'

'Yes, Papa.' Arpita turned towards her room with a fake smile to Bua and waved her hand.

She closed her room's door and began weeping quietly. But even then, she could hear their conversations.

'You are still treating her in that way?! She's not a child anymore, *Bhaiyya* (elder brother). You should let her make her own choices. Let her breathe the air which she deserves, or else, she will die of this torture. She is not *Didi* (elder sister). She is not Ananya!' shouted Mrs Sharma.

'Keep your voice down!' Mr Vyas hissed. 'Arpita is still in her room. And don't tell me how to be a parent. I'm doing this for her. She is my daughter. I won't let anything happen to her. Also, Rekha, you weren't there when all that happened, so you don't have a right to speak to me about this. Keep your mouth shut, especially in front of Arpita. She doesn't have to know any of this.'

Mr Vyas went outside for some fresh air while Mrs Vyas followed him.

Mrs Vyas held her husband's hand. 'Why did you say that to her? You know how sensitive she is. She gets hurt easily, Sudheer.'

'You don't know anything about that night either, Sujata. If you did, you wouldn't be standing here explaining to me. Go. Go inside. I'll be back in a couple of minutes. See what Rekha is doing and make sure to remind her that Arpita needs to stay far away from this topic.'

Mrs Vyas walked back inside with a frowned face and sat right next to Mrs Sharma. No one had a clue that Arpita had listened to most of the conversation and the name of the lady which her Papa and Bua were talking about.

It was around 8 at night. Mr Vyas was very punctual about his schedule and so was Mrs Vyas. The family was done with their dinner. But not Arpita. She was still in her room, trying hard to focus on her studies, but she had an itch about what, rather who they were talking about.

Arpita heard a slight knock on her window, and then her name in a whisper.

Arpita looked closely. There was a shadow behind her window. She grabbed her pen to stab that person.

'Whoever it is, I have a knife. Before I call the cops, run away!' Arpita, while her eyes were closed, hesitantly opened the window, and stopped an inch from stabbing that person.

'Arpita! You could have killed me,' Riya giggled.

'Riya, what are you doing here? Isn't it late for you, too?'

'Arpita, dear, your hands were shaking. You can't even kill a fly. Now move. Let me hop in.' Riya hopped inside her room like a commando does, wearing a pink silk shirt and shorts with boots. 'Okay. Get dressed like the gorgeous girl in Charlie's Angels, because we are going to party!'

'Stop shouting! I can't go. Papa won't let me. Also, all three are sleeping. Sorry, but you must leave, Riya.'

'Honey, I'm not here to go alone. I'm taking you now. I know how you really want to go to the party, so get dressed.'

'No. Papa will find out about this. Believe me. You will get me killed.'

'I have a plan.' Her mischievous smile started giving Arpita goosebumps. 'Your parents won't check on you until tomorrow, and we will be back by 12. Also, we will put some pillows on your bed to make them look like you are sleeping.'

'You know I can't go. If I could, I definitely would. Look, even if you try to consider your option, I'm not sure whether it's going to work or not.'

Riya sat on the floor, making a fake sorrow face, denying going without her. Seeing Riya like that, Arpita had a change of heart.

Riya combined two pillows together in a vertical manner and then covered them with a blanket. To put

cherry on the cake, she placed a black coloured wig on the pillow in the same manner as Arpita in her bed. Meanwhile, Arpita changed her clothes and wore a white top with black jeans with a denim jacket. After looking at Riya's preparation in fooling her parents, 'Wow, Riya! You did well!'

'Shut up. Let's leave and switch off your lights,' said Riya making an annoyed face.

They both left on Riya's scooty. In minutes, they were at the party and Riya drove that scooty like someone was chasing her.

'Wow! Such an amazing party! Come on. Let's dance,' Riya asked Arpita, but she denied it. 'I'm going to get something to fill my belly. I'll dance later.'

Arpita began to eat mostly everything because she never got junk food. She started having fun without Riya. Arpita thought maybe she should go and find Ajay. She had to ask him about his problems. She went on looking for Ajay near the food stall, near the gaming section and even on the dance floor, but he was nowhere to be found.

'Hey, Arpita. I thought Mr Basketball Champion wouldn't let you come, so how are you here?' asked Sameer.

'Hi. Nobody knows that I'm here. Riya bought me here on her dad's Activa. Sameer, have you seen Ajay? I want to talk to him about something.'

'Yeah, he is behind that gaming zone, near the park. And tell him to come dance with me. You look good, Arpita. You should wear this often. Now, enjoy! I'll grab myself a burger. I'm famished.'

'Sure. Thanks, Sameer.' Arpita went around, looking for Ajay by following Sameer's given directions and she saw Ajay smoking and drinking beer.

'Ajay!' Arpita shouted. 'What in the world are you doing here? You know how bad drinking and smoking is for anyone's health. One can die from it. Stop it. Give it to me. You are still drinking and smoking inside the college.'

'So? What is your problem? Huh! Not everyone is like you, Arpita. Oh, sorry, sorry. Topper of every class. You have a perfect life, whereas mine is hell,' Ajay said, tripping over his feet. 'Get lost. Go away. I don't want anyone. Go away like she did. Mrs Mittal, wife of Dhanraj Mittal.'

'What are you talking about? Did your mom leave you? But why?'

'You want to know why?' said Ajay, sipping beer and pointing at the sky. 'She's gone far, far away from me. And you know who took her away? My dad.' Ajay's eyes begin to appear red as if he was going to cry.

'It was raining, and Dad was driving like a maniac while he was drunk. He has been a Hitler my entire life. They hit a tree and puff! Everything got over. My mom's life and mine. If it weren't for my grandma and Bua, I would have run away from that disgusting home, where a murderer lives among us.'

'Ajay, you're drunk. I'm sorry about what happened with your mom. But maybe your dad is also going through the same thing. Maybe you don't know how he feels and might not show it to you.'

Ajay laughed, 'I knew it. You won't believe me. No one does and no one ever will. I am heading home, Arpita. See you tomorrow.'

Ajay tripped over his feet, walked towards his car, and fell right inside, while his driver carefully turned the car around and began its way towards Ajay's home.

'Arpita!' Riya shouted, 'Where have you been? Come on. Let's go home, or your parents might kill me first, then you.'

Riya pushed the start button of her Activa, and Arpita hopped on confusingly. 'Riya, did something happen to Ajay's mom?' asked Arpita doubtfully.

Riya hit the brakes near Arpita's house and asked to never bring this topic up in front of Ajay and told her that she passed away in a car accident, but nobody knew how that accident happened.

'Some say it was rivalry and some say it was a political party's member who made it look like an accident, because Ajay's dad was under some minister, who used to build highways. All I know is, this topic is way more sensitive than any other thing we know. So, do me a favour, Arpita. Let's not talk about it.'

'Sure thing.' Arpita nodded her head and hugged Riya good night and thanked her for all the fun. Riya turned her scooty around and drove off in the blink of an eye. When Arpita reached her main gate, she was shocked. It was around 2 and the lights were on. Suddenly, her calm and peaceful mind started ringing danger bells.

She noticed that her door was unlocked and while entering, all three—Bua, Maa and Papa—were sitting right there on the couch.

In his hoarse voice, Mr Vyas said, 'Sit.' She sat in front of them, staring at the floor and trying to calm herself in the process.

'Where have you been? Do you know what time it is? Answer me now!' her dad asked her, startling Arpita.

She stood up for herself after reorganising the events that had happened during the afternoon.

'Why can't I live my life on my terms?' Arpita shouted while tears began to slowly roll down her cheeks. 'What is it with you? And who is Ananya? I want the truth, and I want you guys to be honest with me.'

Arpita was in fumes and none of her parents or family members has seen her that way. She was crying as well because she was standing up against her Papa for the very first time.

Mr Vyas stood up and went into his room. There was a bit of silence. He came back, handing over a picture to Arpita.

There were three kids in that picture, one boy and two girls.

'The one on the right in your Rekha Bua, in the centre is me and that is your Ananya Bua. She is no more. She was just like you, Arpita. Same height and same nature. Always the best in class and sports. God had sent us a gift. But even the beautiful moon has dark spots. She fell in love with a guy. She was barely 18 and the boy made her take drugs; she started drinking alcohol and other things.'

Rekha Bua interrupted. 'She never stayed the same, her grades started to drop, academics were all in hell. Then, one night, she returned home, crying, and her face was bleeding. She was completely drunk that night. She hung herself to the fan. Just in an instant, she was gone.' Mrs Sharma started crying.

'But Arpita, nobody knows about this. Not even your uncle. So, you shouldn't say anything. Arpita, I know I have been very hard on you but–'

'It's okay, Papa. I know now, and I'm sorry, but you have to understand, too. I can't always be dependent on you or ask for your permission. I know I won't do any such thing like Ananya Bua. You have to trust me on that and count on me. Have faith in your teachings and blessings, please. I should go to bed, and I won't do any kind of running away like this. But please promise me as well you will try to let me do things my way as well,' said Arpita.

'Yes dear, I promise you. We all should get some rest now. Good night, everyone.' Everyone walked into their rooms and closed the door.

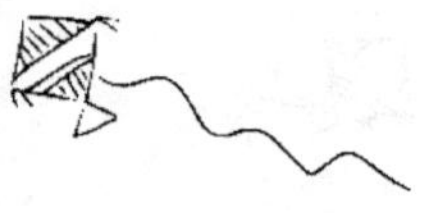

The Path Towards Destiny

Sayani Halder

An eye on the goal will automatically
bring you closer to destiny.

The path towards the goal
May lead to hardships and sacrifices,
But the result will be breath-taking
with lots of joy and achievements.

Alliance

Pranav Uberoi

We, humans, tend to draw
inspiration from the blackholes
of our life.
It's the delusion we live in.

Our strength begins to grow
with the mere glimmer of hope.
Yet we live in our past rather than
present, and future seems relevantly
irrelevant.

Our capabilities and abilities
push us to the limits of our
humanly strength, but we seek
shed under the umbrella of inspiration.

Don't bend the rules, they are
for your protection.
Inspiration doesn't seem to play
by rules,
I suppose. Or did I misinterpret
it. Should I apologise?

Alliance with inspiration has
been done but the terms and
conditions, blurry they sound,
Signature forged with a smile
tends to seal the deal.

The more we show strength,
inspiration serves us yet a fickle
doubt in ourselves draws it away to
a land distant, never to be seen
again.

Se7en Ligaments

Pranav Uberoi

Destruction.
Devastated.
Delusional.
Dysfunctional.
Disintegrated.
Distorted.
Diverse.

These words seem to
sound, mean, hear something
same, some not. Some of them
dilute your inner strength, some
crush your bones and let you
know, you are just millions of
sand particles put together.

You wish to run away
with your arms stretched up, trying
to connect with the sky that's beyond
your reach but eyes closed
keeping you in a state of delusion.

The destruction within you
disintegrates your mind and
your inability to process your
hearts voices seem to make
you distort.

You walk on paths of
misery, blind slighted by
your faith in the protection
by the ultimate protector.
Is it dysfunctional thinking
or vicious downfall?

Diversity presents itself in
forms you wouldn't like to see it,
It's not cultural, regional, language
It's something out of words
and beyond your despair,
thinking and false courage.

Falling Recklessly

Pranav Uberoi

I have been falling recklessly
over the messages I wish to
receive from someone
with whom I sort of lost connection.

I have been falling recklessly
over my future, which is somewhere
lost, and my present is seeking survival.

I have been falling recklessly
over the chats which were once
somewhat alive but now they are
vague memories.

I have been falling recklessly
over my creativity, wish I could
polarise its essence in me, if someday,
someone doubts it, I would know
where to fall.

I have been falling recklessly
over my dreams, they have
been overwhelming, yet
the reality of those is nowhere close.

I have been falling recklessly
Over certain emotions, they have
been misleading but the possibility
of turning into reality would
be based on presumptions.
I have been falling recklessly
over my eagerness to put the
right things in perspective, yet
my mind deceives me from
being a better version of me.

Thread

Pranav Uberoi

Have our fingers met, have our fingers
touched each other's fingertips.
As it seems we never
inclined into each other's fate
But to the thread which makes
us believe in "us".

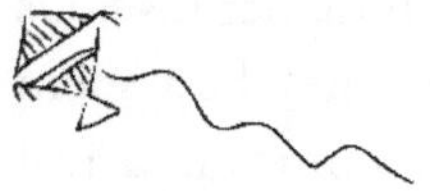

The Real Treasure

Sandhita Agarwal

The skin on his face felt itchy. The frostbite had set in. His hands felt numb under his thick mittens. He could see the peak now. A white, glacial, scary pinnacle, almost obscured by a dark, grey cumulonimbus cloud. The brutal wind assaulted his visage, and he pulled his blue parka hood tighter over his head. *This was worth it,* he thought to himself. He resumed his arduous climb to the top.

The lore of the ancient mountain had been handed down from generation to generation. His grandfather had often told him stories about the people who surmounted the harsh, merciless mountain and found untold treasures at the top. They all came back rich, happy, and fulfilled. But their lips were sealed. It was the rule of the mountain. The one condition for its eternal magnanimity. It couldn't be broken. But for every person that made out alive, thousands quit, and hundreds died. It was for that reason that the mountain was often called "Le Tueur Blanc".

It was the fifteenth day of his ascent. He had set up camp in a small crevice in the mountain. He lay in his sleeping bag, bundled up in numerous layers of clothing. He was out of the storm, but the cold was unappeasable. He grabbed a candy bar from his pack and started munching on the hard chocolate. He couldn't taste it. His mouth felt frozen and dry. As he closed his eyes, the scene before his eyes shifted rapidly, from the dark, icy cave ceiling to a lush green meadow. The sun shone brightly, and the air was redolent with the scent of lavender flowers. She lay next to him, her luscious jet-black hair spread in a halo around her face. They had spent many afternoons like that, sneaking out of their homes and just lying next to each other. But it had all come to an end when her brother, the village chief, had discovered their budding romance. The night was etched into his mind as clearly as the face of his mother. He, the son of a poor woodcutter, had dared to love the chief's sister. It was that night that he had decided that he would either return home, victorious with the treasures from the death mountain, or perish. That was a year ago.

The next days on the mountain were agonising. There was no respite from the cold and the storm. The winds got stronger and at one precarious juncture, the wind barrelled against him, and he almost lost his footing and would have fallen 200 feet to his death. The mountain felt like a living and breathing entity, a tempestuous and wrathful god. Every day when he woke up, there were ice crystals on his cheeks. He had started crying in his sleep. He longed for his mother and her warm, comforting meals. He yearned for the delicious soup his mother made, the meat in the hearty broth always melting on his tongue. Some days, he felt like quitting and returning home. Shameful but alive. But then, Anoyekani's face would pop into his mind. If she married someone else, he would die anyway, and so, he trudged on.

On the 26th night of his journey, he saw his dead grandmother. He was setting up camp for the night on a flat, white plain. For the first time, it was quiet on the mountain. It was as if the mountain had prepared a show for him. There was an electric buzz in the air. It scared him. He was just climbing into his tent when he saw the apparition 10 feet away. It was his dead grandmother in her burial clothes. He stood rooted to the spot. A second passed by, and she melted right in front of his eyes into a white mist that hung in the air for a few seconds and was then carried away by the winds. His heart was beating rapidly in his chest, and he could finally move. He quickly got into the tent and zipped it up. He was surely seeing things. He had never heard of ghosts on the mountain. He couldn't get to sleep the whole night.

It was the final day of his journey. He knew he would make it. He *would* live to see his mother again. He was nearing the final ascent. With a huge heave, he pulled himself to the summit. He lay there at the top of the white monolith, his heart beating in his chest, and the gales bellowing in his face. He cautiously got to his feet and looked around the frozen tundra. The roaring winds blurred his vision, but he walked around the expanse of the summit. It was empty and bare. Where was the treasure? Had the treasures finally been depleted? Was the mountain finally dead? Did he have to dig? He knew for a fact that none of the people who came to the mountain carried gears for any sort of excavation. His heart began to sink. He felt cheated. Maybe the treasure was buried after all. He had risked his life for nothing, and he might die on his way down. He sat down with his head in his hands and cried, his tears freezing instantly on his ragged face.

His life started flashing in front of him. His childhood, his adolescence, and his youth. The people that he loved, the people that he forgot, and the people that he lost. And as he sat there in the cold darkness of dejection and failure, something started to happen inside him. A warmth began to spread from the deepest realms of his heart, outwards, towards his extremities. It slowly engulfed his whole body, and he felt warm! His mind began to explode with visions of the stories that the mountain whispered into his ears. He saw them, the people before him, and he saw their wisdom. He saw them work tirelessly in preparation for the climb. He watched them leave behind weeping families with stony resolves in their tender hearts. He felt their tenacity when every slip on the mountain made them feel like quitting, and yet, they soldiered on. He saw his journey reflected in their lives. And at last, he understood. He finally comprehended the secret of the mountain. He felt his eyes brim with tears, but this time, their warmth gave him comfort. He smiled as he thanked the mountain for the real treasure he had discovered and slowly made his way back down the now calm mountainside.

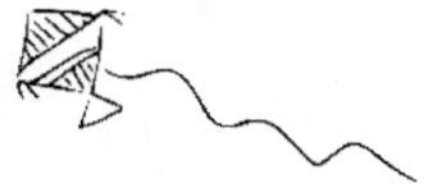

Adoption

Ashley Sanchez

Unplanned doesn't mean unwanted or unloved.
It just means life brought something I needed before I ever knew.
It was never easy knowing it will be me
Acknowledging that it could be difficult to be a mom
Nine months growing was the best thing that I looked forward to
Not knowing that it would sadden me to do it all on my own
Everyday raised doubt and even a question about moving on
I was only 17 and had a lot to learn
However, each day I woke up admiring him and loving every baby move
I cried several times asking myself if I could be a mom
I always thought that maybe he would be better off with someone else
I knew that many people were out there who wanted to give that love

To cherish and guide a child with all they could

I declined abortion as I knew I couldn't live knowing that
I did that to my own son

All because I wasn't ready or to please someone else

Adoption was an option that I thought of very much

but when I gave birth, I knew I was a mom.

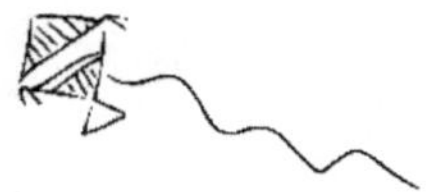

Tears

Ashley Sanchez

It took one instant to see my son tear up as he saw me ball up.

His little face with tears made it worse for me as he came up to me to hug me tightly.

When I cry, he cries, and I had no idea that could be…

Sometimes, we think our children are too small to even see what we have going on.

However, we are all human and share emotions that cannot be undone.

He always notices when I'm sad and asks me, 'Mommy, what's wrong?'

As sensitive as I am, it's hard for me to hide and pretend nothing's wrong.

So, I took it upon myself to cry outside, in my vehicle, or
anywhere far away from his sight

Because no child deserves to see their mommy in such a way or
even at their lowest of them all.

I cry because I feel devastated.

I stress because I feel overwhelmed.

At times, I feel all I do isn't enough.

I take my moments to let it all out, I yell and scream
and recover from it

to avoid him seeing mommy in her tears

and to come back home smiling for him.

Winner

Garv Archana

I might not be useful,
not a thing to cherish.
My extroverted side
may soon perish.

Something I am,
Yet I'm nothing.
All I wish is
to be at least something.

My existence is limited to
inhaling and exhaling.
Have I even got a purpose
On this blue dot rotating?

I want to be bigger
than this form I inhabit.
Graduating towards it
daily a bit.

The efforts I make,
Won't let go in vain.
Acceptable for it,
Tad some pain.

One day, I'll rise
and outshine all.
No one can stop
My victory call.

I'll win my battles and
oust them out.
'Hail the winner,'
Everyone will shout!

Determined

Neeraja Krishnaswami

Each one of us is unique,
Each one of us is different.

Each one of us has our own battles to face.

Each one of us has a different way to
deal with our struggles.

It is important to remember
that we can face it head along,
individually and by being together,
if we are determined.

Neither is any goal unattainable
nor should we undermine ourselves
or demotivate others
by calling each other underachievers.

Advice for some
A reiteration for
others

This may seem.

Let's face it!
Face the fact!

Let's not get buried
in the deepest of our worries
and forget to enjoy
our strength, our today!

By the Sea

Siddhi Chouthai

I sit by the shore staring at the waves beneath me,
Trying to take in the sparkling vastness ahead of me.
One by one the mighty waves crash against the lands,
Making splashes that calm me somehow.

It seems like the sea talks to me
As it hits the shore incessantly.
The gravel and the boulders can stop it not
As it makes its path in all adversities.
Will not give up, will not give in
Scream the waves seemingly,
So is this beautiful element of the natural realm.

The rivers and streams tired by the journey,
Seek shelter in the lap of the sea,
From tiny creatures to humongous reeds
All are fostered by thee.

As a mother takes in the beloved child close to
her bosom and puts to sleep,
So tomorrow, it can start with new vigour and leap.

Be bold, be free just like the harmonious sea,
Hesitate not to hit new shores and tread new paths.
Even if the storms visit, they can never last.
The calm waters will always triumph at last.
Be beautiful, let the sunlight seep in,
to highlight sparkling strengths,
And its shimmer lasting even on the darkest nights.

The breeze passes like a mysterious stranger,
telling me the tales of the waves coming along.
The restless sea is also serene.
The white tides come again with more energy.
Where do they come from? Where do they retreat?
I wonder as I get lost in this serendipity.

If I can rise, If I can see
myself changing into a better me,
just like this mighty sea.
Admiring the tireless efforts ahead of me,
and how I love sitting by it.

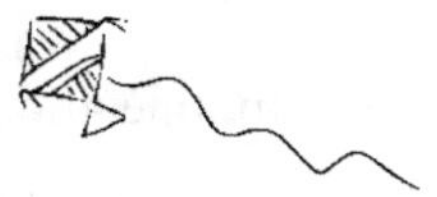

The Reflection

Apoorva Ravi

She looked at herself in the mirror. She saw a stranger whom she didn't want to identify with. She was not that fat person she saw. She was a dancer, athletic, vibrant, and full of life. She did not know who this zombie was, who had to take antidepressants so that she was normal according to doctors.

Huh, normal! Well, what is normal—the ones who do everything according to the norm? But who sets these norms anyway? Just some human who wanted to control everyone around them. But well, who cares?

The dancer who danced did not care. She was happy. She was thin. She was beautiful. Not fat like her. So, who was she?

'Athira!'

'Yes, Amma.' Athira blinked. Her thoughts had taken hold of her again. 'Well, you are not beautiful so just stop dreaming!' Athira told the mirror and went to the hall.

'Athira, when will you exercise? Look how much weight you have gained. It's just not healthy.'

Oh! Here we go again. She is back at it, thought Athira and rolled her eyes.

'I saw that, Athira. Why don't you understand? You may get diabetes. You are taking these medicines. You need to exercise. You just don't listen!'

'Aaargh! Why doesn't she just get it? I am tired of it. I don't like being told to do something. I will do it when I feel like it. Not when she tells me!'

Ruffling her hair, she went to the balcony with her mobile and earphones. 'Autumn days that dawn your face...

You can be reckless like birds in the sky Wherever you go...'

Ah! Closing her eyes, the lyrics of the Otherside by Birdy playing on her mobile brought that smile which her mother would have been so happy to see. But well, it was only solitude that gave her happiness and peace.

Thud, thud, thud! She saw someone on the other balcony, dancing! But wait! She was not thin. She was not like those thin dancers, but still, she looked so beautiful. She looked so happy. Athira was mesmerised. Unknown to her, her feet started moving to the beats of the music and there—she felt it—she felt like the carefree, vibrant dancer that she wanted to be. It was magical!

'Hey!' Athira turned. 'You dance so well!' It was the girl. She had seen her dance. And she had said it was good!

'I have a community dance space. Do you want to come?'

Athira hesitated. Others would be there. Would it be okay? Would they laugh? Well, who cares! She wanted to dance and that was it and she would not worry what others think.

'Athira!'

'Yes, Amma!' came a joyous reply.

As she came downstairs, her mother was surprised and overwhelmed. She had not seen her daughter so happy for a long time. She did not know what had happened on the terrace. But her daughter's smile was all that she cared about.

That night, Athira looked at herself in the mirror. She saw the vibrant dancer smiling at her. And she was home.

Sunshine

Sree Yelamanchi

Slaying the daunting darkness,
Sparkling through the mesmerising skies,
Skimming the blooming sepals,
Singing with the perched songbirds,
Scattering upon the crowded city blocks,
Seeping through the cracked windows,
The glory rays of sunshine,
Soothing her stretched eyes,
Stroking her strung-out soul,
Silencing the havoc in her heart
with the hope of a new dawn!

Bare Feet

Sree Yelamanchi

The little girl in white,
curly hair looping with the mellow wind,
bare feet kissing the dewy grass,
blue eyes shining under the saffron skies,
velvety hands brushing the tender vines,
springing with a glee unfettered,
shadowing the adrift dandelion,
her spirit alike soaring free and wild,
steering to the zenith no fret in the wide world,
like the little girl in white!

Fallen Soul

Sree Yelamanchi

Astray in a woodland
through the rocky wind trudging,
Eyes jaded and wrists bleeding
Arduous feet dragging on,
Forging ahead onto the quest for
Her truant fallen soul,
Courage undeterred alone left
Credence unshattered only spared,
Scars the solely adornments
Strewing the path ablaze,
Tailing the light into the wilderness,
She trod the path forbidden,
heart bearing vigour and resilience!

These Are Here To

Shreya Chauhan

This society is just here to judge you.
You should know that you're born for stars.
Nothing, not even you can hold yourself back.
Just go ahead and make a move!

These failures are here to teach you,
To teach you what success actually means.
Let these failures be your scars,
Who just add to your beauty of success!

These scars are here to tell everyone,
That you're brave and you fought bravely.
These are an important part of you.
Don't let them fade!

These flaws in you are here to make you realise,
that besides these you also carry perfections.
Without these, you won't ever realise,
that you're yet to be perfect!

So just keep everything aside
And crave for stars and beyond.

You’re A Precious Gem

Shreya Chauhan

They hurt you?
It’s okay, don’t sit and cry. This will just prove ‘em you’re weak.
But you yourself know you’re not.
Just show them that you’re more powerful than
they imagined you to be.

They hit you?
Just don’t hit them back in return
Become independent and successful.
They will then get a hard slap.

They forgot you?
Then don’t stay with them. Don’t give importance to those
who can’t even remember you!
Just find you in yourself because you would not forget you
in the wildest of dreams.

They beg you?
Now see, they are the people who did bad to you.
Let people call you an egoist but just don't accept their begging.
They beg for you because you're a precious gem,
no one wants to lose.

Remember that you're a precious gem!

I Am Depressed and I Am a Great Mom

Monica Dedich

It's been a few rough weeks at home. I was back to working full time, my husband was working overtime seven days a week, and our two little munchkins needed the same amount of attention. Navigating my return to work with two kids and having to do so when my husband was unavailable to support me, something not his choice, has been hard on me. I did not expect it to be this challenging, and now, a few weeks later, I feel like I am running on empty. I am tired. I am stressed, and I am anxious. I am irritable. And I am vulnerable.

Depression has moved back in with me—in my chest, where I feel the weight of it all crushing me, forcing me to take shallow breaths; in my head, where it shelters thoughts of inadequacy and failure; and in my heart, where it breeds a hybrid venom of anger, resentment, and sadness.

Yet, I feel rebellious, even in those moments where I feel worthless, fatigued by it all. Through the tears, I can hear a voice within me, rising, but louder each time: I am done with your lies, depression. I have less and less patience for your agonising torment. For your house of mirrors with warped reflections of who I am.

I feel a revolution brewing inside of me. It is feeble, but it's there. I am not falling for depression's tricks as easily anymore. It's like a baby, taking its very first steps: tentative, ungraceful, bound to fall flat on its face now and again. Not knowing when it will all come together to form some coordinated sequence of movements.

But it's happening. What I thought never would. Depression losing its grip on me. It still has its clutches around my neck, and it will take more time to break free and shake it off, maybe never completely. Yet, I feel lighter already. My throat has enough wiggle room to, at the very least, whisper my truth, and not what depression would have me see as reality. I find myself in a bizarre, awkward yet empowering space, where I am both strong and drained, aware, and confused.

I am a phenomenal mother. I am a flawed mother.

I don't know if this is the beginning of the end of my depression. I don't know if it will ever be truly gone. Vanquished, like the dragons of old. I have no idea how this will all work out for me. But I know that I will be here.

A phenomenal mother through it all.

Maybe I need to say this more for my benefit than to prove anything to others. I am still here, day in and day out, doing my absolute best and my everything to raise my children. Some days (most days), my best is far from picture perfect. But I am the best mother my kids could ever ask for. I am good at it, even on my worst days.

I'm *great* at it.

Despite my depression. In the face of every ounce of self-doubt I have ever experienced.

I am a phenomenal mother.

I am drained. I am overwhelmed. I am strong. I am resilient.

I feel weak. I feel dejected. I am reborn. I am rising.

These can and do coexist in the same space. I can be grateful for my beautiful babies and feel anxiety at being alone with them at home without another set of hands to help. I can appreciate the precious moments where my baby girl cuddles up to me and feel like the next time I drive past the airport, I might hop on a plane to Fiji with a one-way ticket.

Somehow, we have fallen into this trap of absolutes: you are either depressed and therefore somehow incapable of feeling gratitude for your privileges and good fortune. Or your mental health is peachy, and you are smiling from ear to ear through motherhood.

Living with mental illness is not an absolute condition. While my brain might be going through some shit and sending me warped messaging because of it, it is not *broken*. I am not broken. I have broken days. Moments. And sometimes, they line up together to form an excessively long sequence.

But I am still here. And I can finally see my depression in its true form: a slave driver to my state of mind. To my needs and wants, cracking its whip at my self-esteem.

I am in a state of transition these days, which I suspect is part of the reason why I feel out of sorts. Change is good. Rising from my own ashes is great. But it is not yet a complete process.

I am just barely, tentatively liberated. There is a renewed sense of power flowing through me. And I am slowly, steadily learning to embrace it and let it lead my way.

I can't get the image of a child learning to take their first steps, and, ironically, my daughter is at precisely that moment in her young life. I see myself in her stumbles and tumbles, though I get the sense she will figure out her path much quicker than I will.

But I am tingling with excitement to work through it.

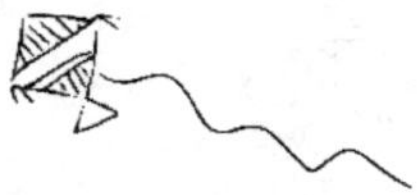

You

Parleen Kaur Oberoi

I'll hold on to your dulcet voice
On days when I'm not strong
I'll believe I'm your choice
During nights awfully long.

I'll hold on to your every word
In times when I can't remember myself
Reminiscing every storm, we incurred
Your imposing lack of stealth.

I'll hold on to our every embrace
Every minute I fall apart
Savouring your every trace
Lost in the abyss of my heart.

Her

Parleen Kaur Oberoi

Her words
Stronger than my latte
Nonetheless, reside
Someplace in my notes.
She who had
A soul so genuine
A touch so cosy
Which swept my heart away
Every moment
I sit with myself
Realisation hits,
How deserted I am
Devoid her.
Someone like her
Lovely and sunny
Yet so hardcore.

Near to the heart,
Yet so distant.
If tears could bring you back
And pain could build a highway
I would ache a thousand years for you.
'Cause you, my friend
Have taught me
How it is
To have loved and lost.
To find everything you wished for
in a person, someone who breathes home.
Someone I miss.

Hope

Parleen Kaur Oberoi

Where did your gleam of hope go,
In the midst of trying times?
Who robbed you of that bewitching beam,
Dishevelled, leery to whine
While the dark days loomed around you,
And you grappled hard?
Your obstinate self awaited a fresh start.
Now I ask you to hold on
Hang on to those shackles just a while more
'Cause you can't be hindered
Not until you're you,
The riotous you.

Need

Parleen Kaur Oberoi

And in sleepless nights like these
When all my demons arouse
Is it unfair to seek
The tone of a voice that can put me to rest
Expressions that offer me consolation
Maybe dreams that beckon me?
For all I know, there's dusk in me,
Still lingering,
Aspiring a dawn
Redeem me before this, too, is gone.

Those Inner Voices

Parleen Kaur Oberoi

Those days when I sat alone
And gazed at the stars that shone
Someone said it's time to sleep
Someone said, 'Why didn't you weep?'
For the loss of mine was hard to bear
And no kind words left to hear.

Something inside pulled me down.
Something inside kicked that crown.
My lips were dry, forced to keep mum
But many a sad song my heart did hum.

But time will fly, even if you cry
And then came the sunrise
Which woke me up to life
It just wasn't a battle I lost
But a lesson learnt with very high a cost
Sometimes you need to step out of that shell
And shout to yourself, 'All will be well.'

A Tale of Two

Claire Casapao

An incredulous whisper of 'He can't be dead, can he?' Melancholy violin music starts playing—it sounds like fingernails scratching a blackboard. 'He is.'

The confirmation of their worst fears hits them like a truck.

Years Earlier

The sun rises high in the sky, streaking the clouds with gold and orange. Loud trumpet noises play.

Panting.

Shouts of 'Faster!'

A recruit lags the large crowd of others ahead.

He can't run any faster.

He can't run any further.

But he keeps going.

Every day, until he gets stronger. His resolve never wavers.

Night

The recruit is wide awake. He wonders who could sleep through his bunkmates' loud snoring. Certainly not him.

He thinks of his family, far away from him. He remembers his old life.

He remembers why he's there, stretched out over a bed in the barracks of the military academy. He wants to protect his country.

The recruit is still wide awake. He sneaks down from the bed, trying not to wake anyone up.

Push ups were horrible for him. *I'm going to change that,* he thought.

Two hundred push ups later, the recruit decides to get some rest. Tiptoeing softly back to his bed, he trips over a loose floorboard.

Footsteps.

The recruit runs.

Day

'You are soldiers, not lazy rats. You must be able to endure all kinds of conditions. Most importantly, you must not give up. You are here to protect your country.'

The recruits are running once more.

This recruit is still stumbling. He's falling apart. He's sweating uncontrollably. He can't keep going. He has to stop.

He falls down. Down, down, down. He feels traumatised. He feels panicked.

He'll never be able to make it. He's not good enough. His subconscious swirls with these thoughts.

He'll never be enough. He can't do it. He has to pack up and go home and face the exultation of all those people who said he wouldn't make it.

Horrifying deprecating remarks fly through the recruit's mind. He doesn't notice anything else. He doesn't notice how much faster he runs than he used to. He doesn't notice he's starting to catch up.

But his head is spinning. He has to continue. He can't stop. He's weak.

'Keep going, faster, faster!' yells the drill sergeant.

The recruit pulls himself out of his subconscious back into the sunshine—into the real world. He finally notices the light in what he believes to be darkness.

Last day

The recruit…the valedictorian. He is the best. He has the best endurance. He is the strongest.

He has never forgotten how he used to be—the weak, stuttering, and stumbling recruit. 'Kid, why don't you become a drill sergeant?'

'I don't like yelling at people, Sir.'

'Nonsense. We don't just yell at people, we motivate them.' 'I still don't want to.'

'So, you're going to join the army? You want to fight?' 'Yes, Sir.'

'They need someone like you, now that they've declared war.'

War

The recruit is now a soldier.

Bullets are flying from all directions. Bodies fall onto the mud, lifeless.

He didn't want to be one of them.

He fought hard and bravely for his country. He sacrificed a normal civilian life.

He thought of this—it propelled him to keep fighting.

A bullet rushes past him and hits the soldier next to him on the chest. The soldier shoots the opposing army's commander on the neck.

The battle was won.

More battles. More victories.

The soldier rises through the ranks.

He becomes the General of the army.

His troops fight through the war under his leadership. It seems as if they will emerge victorious.

Until tragedy strikes.

Final Night

The general's body lay on the floor, still and cold, with a bullet embedded in his chest. The walls and floor were spattered with thick, dark red blood.

Those walls were the only witness to the fatal deed.

A tall man had snuck into the general's room in the middle of the night. The general had been fast asleep.

He was oblivious to the heavy footsteps approaching his bed. The tall man slowly drew a revolver out of his pocket and shot him.

The general's dead body rolled off the bed, onto the floor where it lay, silent and unmoving until the sunrise.

The next morning

The general's soldiers found a piece of paper on his nightstand. A letter from his wife. It only contained one sentence.

'War is a living hell—end it. By that, I mean, win it.'

Present day

The miserable mood is infectious. 'He was a great man!' exclaims a woman passionately. 'He had a family! He had a promising career! My poor little boy,' sobs the general's mother. His widow attempts to console her.

'He's not your little boy anymore—he's grown up to be a man—

a protector. He protects all of us. We haven't all been wiped out yet because of his courage. We've even won the war! He died for a cause he believed in, and that's something to be proud of.'

A tall, thin black shadow appears at the gates of the cemetery. It's the general's murderer.

More tragedy

The murderer is wearing a dark cloak and hood, obscuring his features. He is carrying a revolver—the same one that killed the general.

The taste of revenge becomes sweeter as he approaches the melancholy party.

No one notices him—their tears cloud their vision. It is evident to the murderer that this will be easy—as easy as assassinating the general.

Gunshots ring through the air, one after the other. Each one is punctuated by a scream and a thud. Soon, the murderer is facing the last person alive. The general's widow.

He slowly pulls off his hood.

He's the drill sergeant.

'Why are you doing this?' she demands.

'It's not fit for ugly little housewives like you to know my reasons,' snarled the drill sergeant. 'The phrase "ugly little housewives" does not include me—for one, I was a spy for the military. Our military. And you know you're just jealous of my husband's success.'

'Jealous, am I?'

Flashback

The drill sergeant is sitting in his room with the general—a recruit back then. 'Kid, why don't you become a drill sergeant?'

'I don't like yelling at people, Sir.'

'Nonsense. We don't just yell at people, we motivate them.' 'I still don't want to.'

'So, you're going to join the army? You want to fight?' 'Yes, Sir.'

'They need someone like you, now that they've declared war.' 'Sir, can you have a family and still be a soldier?'

'I heard that there are benefits for married soldiers in the army—only our army, to bait people into joining. Why do you ask?'

'Just asking.'

With this, the recruit gets up and returns to the barracks.

A year after this conversation, before the recruit joined the army, he married the drill sergeant's younger sister. His only sister.

For his own personal gain.

He wanted to get the benefits married soldiers did in their army. He didn't love her.

So, she joined the army as a spy. Secretly, while pretending to be a housewife, just to get closer to him.

Or so her brother thought.

Present day

'I hate to call you my brother,' whispered the widow, softly.

'Can't you see? He would never love you, you desperate, naïve brat! He was using you! I don't want to see you running around like a little dog!' he screamed.

'And I didn't join the army just to get close to him, you old bag! I wanted to protect my country, just

as he did!'

The widow's patience had finally reached its end. She yanked the revolver out of her brother's hands and pointed it at him.

'Your own brother?' asks the drill sergeant, laughing.

'The brother who doesn't even know my name!' she screeches. 'The brother who insulted my family! The brother who murdered innocent people! Just because he thought I needed saving! I'm not a damsel in distress, you know! And I'm more than what you think I am! I'm stronger than you think! I'm not that little girl who sobbed uncontrollably when she fell on her face anymore!'

She pulls on the trigger.

The last gunshot had been fired.

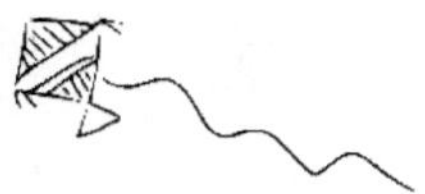

Acknowledgements

I'd like to take this opportunity to thank the publishing house for supporting me in this venture and helping me achieve this feat. It would never be possible without your support. The next would be my wings, my co-authors who have been very patient and my backbone in this. This couldn't have happened without you. Finally, I'd like to thank and seek the blessings of my family, who have been my torch bearers for the right path time and again. I hope to never let you down.

Let's meet the writers of this Anthology.

Soumya Tewari

Soumya is a marketing professional who often finds her solace in the world of words. She is a published co-author and a passionate poet and blogger who believes in the magic of simple moments and loves compiling them into meaningful stories. You can connect with her on Instagram @poetrusic_sam.

Monica Dedich

Monica, a.k.a. Mother in Progress, is a multicultural mutt based in Canada. A mother of two, she is a postpartum depression survivor and writes about motherhood's struggles and truths with honest vulnerability. You can find more of her writings on: momoinprogress.medium.com

Garv Archana

The author is a 10th grader, living in Varanasi, the oldest inhabited city and the land of Malaiyyo. He first picked up the pen when he was 9. Glad to his poor memory that he forgot to put it down. Cooking up poems and stories with his ladle of emotions is the craft with which he feeds people. A craft which has his sincerest efforts of satiating peoples' hearts. Enjoy his work on Instagram @noob_garvv.

Anju Gupta

Anju Gupta is a seasoned education industry leader and self-cultivator. She has excelled in the field of writing. Her views have been published in print and digital media and recognised on various platforms. Her poetic pieces are based on hard facts and challenging experiences of life and hit deep into the hearts of readers/listeners. Her writing and narration acumen has been applauded by one and all.

Ritu Ambwani

Ritu hails from Bhilai, Chhattisgarh, and pursued Engineering in Electrical and Electronics. A content writer by day in an e-commerce FMCG company and a passionate writer by night. When she is not writing and sipping tea in her favourite outlet, Ritu spends most of her time reading and watching documentaries. She believes that reading can change the world and uses it to inspire young people.

Vaishnavi Kulkarni

A cheerful girl from Hubli, Vaishnavi is a B. A. student in SJMVS Women's College. She is someone who likes to use her moves to free her mind. She also relies on calming herself down with amazing songs. She dreams to heal wounded souls in the future as a counsellor. This shows her golden heart and its beauty better.

Aditya Jhingan

Aditya recognised his passion for writing a bit late in his life, but still, with all his imagination, observation skills, and daydreaming, he manages to write his heart out on the paper. His tone of writing is always in a way that everyone can read, understand, and feel the stories. He keeps his writing simple and neat. Apart from being a writer, Aditya is passionate about cooking, watching plenty of movies and TV shows to gain a new perspective on how a particular show was written or performed, and the fun fact is, he learnt his English speaking and writing by watching all those movies he admired.

Kashish Lewis

Currently in Bangalore, Kashish Lewis is a poet, author, and designer. You will find her at a local bookstore, open mics, cafes or simply rummaging through a stack of books on sale. She talks about mental health, modern-day feminism and other social issues on her social media pages. Her love for meeting people and learning from new connections brings her to the world of events. Find her debut poetry book "You Me and Love" on Amazon or the Inkfeathers Bookstore. Connect with her on Instagram @k.writesofficial or on LinkedIn @KashishLewis.

Pranav Uberoi

Pranav Uberoi is 26 years old, born and brought up in New Delhi. His writing journey started when he was in second grade by writing greeting cards. Writing has presented him with opportunities that he could not believe. His writings are appreciated and binged by many.

Neeraja Krishnaswami

Neeraja Krishnaswami is a post-graduate in Business Management, an Accounts Executive with her father, and a blogger by choice. Writing being her passion, she has participated in poetry and story writing competitions and is a co-author in anthologies. Apart from writing, her hobbies are singing, painting, and landscape photography. She can be contacted through her IG handles @neerajak_94 and @nkaysfictionalparadise.

Sandhita Agarwal

Sandhita is a software developer by profession but a hippie at heart. She likes to travel the world and meet different people. She is one of the authors showcased in the anthology Minds@Work2. She lives with her spunky cocker spaniel in Bangalore and hopes to have a tête-à-tête with Salman Rushdie one day.

Manish M Nair

Manish is a production engineer by profession from Pune. He writes short stories and poems on versatile genres. He also likes to sing and draw. For him, writing is to re-create the reality. You can find him on Instagram @accu_qua.man.

Shreya Chauhan

Apart from being a student and a 17-year-old, Shreya is an avid reader. Her favourite genres are fiction and murder mystery. A writer, here and there, on this and that, who writes what she reads and feels. Other than reading, she likes to sing and learn new languages.

Tanisha Sharma

Tanisha is a 21-year-old hyperactive person, who currently spends most of her time in contemplating her life and future. Though all this writing is her greatest escape from reality, she's a science student with kinks of philosophy and literature, and nothing can cheer her more than a young adult/romance novel and a strong cold coffee.

Apoorva Ravi

Apoorva is a writer, poet, and mental health advocate. With live experience in the field of mental health, she wants to spread awareness in the field. She is also a PhD scholar, music enthusiast, and loves her cats and dogs a lot.

Ishita Sharma

Ishita Sharma was born on 10th January 2006 in Jaipur, Rajasthan. She is pursuing her hobby of writing since she was fifteen years of age and is doing her official writing debut through this book. She writes against social evils, and she is a feminist, too. She is inspired by the great poet Manoj Muntashir who wrote many prominent poems.

Ashley Sanchez

Ashley with a second name Icela is a young mom who, above her struggles, continues to conquer the world as best as she can. Writing has been her coping mechanism to fight against all other emotions involved. She writes about her personal experiences mostly; however, it is often that she also likes placing herself in others' shoes to be able to express the pain others may be feeling as well. 'Oftentimes, we find ourselves only noticing what's on the outside or what people portray. We never know the reality of things and writing to survive makes me feel I can help someone else survive if not today, tomorrow, or the next day.'

Samresh Mahapatra

Samresh—a kid lost in his own wonderland, a utopian land where he finds his ikigai in himself. He is a complete mystery box of creations which can get you butterflies and giggles at the same time. Conversations can range from international politics and rocket science to gossips about the girl in the red dress who just crossed your path. He is always up for conversations even at midnight, sorting tons of issues, but when this facility comes with a warning, he can sleep legit anywhere on earth, be it the single sofa or the front seat of a speeding bike.

Siddhi Chouthai

Siddhi is a voracious reader. Exploring the world of books made her understand her command over writing. She inclines her thoughts on matters as they strike her, shaping them into philosophical angles, stories, and poems. Her strong genre of interest is mythology. Other pursuits that come to her are that of values, morals and motivation. Apart from writing, Siddhi is an artist. She paints and sketches with lucidity. She is a passionate dancer, Bharatnatyam being her forte and western freestyle being her interest. Her other interests being sports and watching TV series and movies with perceptive mind. She has received ample accolades for her mentioned fields.

Parleen Oberoi

A proud army brat, Parleen Oberoi is currently an undergraduate at Dell Technologies, and though the job is technical, she loves the realms of fantasy. When she is not sleeping, she's found reading or binging a Spanish show. For her, poetry is catharsis. Parleen will be graduating from SRM University, Chennai in BTech (Computer Science) by June this year.

Sayani Halder

Sayani Halder is a 23-year-old girl. She lives in Kolkata, West Bengal. She completed her graduation from Kazi Nazrul University with an honour's degree in sociology and is currently pursuing Master's in Sociology from Rabindra Bharati University. She is also working in Railway Childline under the designation of a Counsellor. Her favourite leisure activity is to listen to music, read books, crafting, etc. She is a very energetic, bubbly, and hardworking girl and can adapt to any environment around her.

Michael Tucker

Michael Tucker is a 25-year-old man from Scotland. He has performed poetry at the fringe festival and a member of International Association of Professional Writers and Editors.

Shreya Halder

An artist at heart, Shreya paints her words with much effort. She takes time to patiently carve her piece to perfection before the world reads. She is an engineer who is here to live a beautiful day with her complete positivity. She is a firm yet sensitive ice cream lover who craves it at the worst times you'd expect. Shreya is a woman always lost in the arms of nature. Walk a mile with her and you will find her.

Sree Yelamanchi

A doctor by profession and a writer by passion who chose writing to get through the dark days of her life, Sree eventually fell in love with it, and she now believes it's the pen that chooses the one. Books, coffee, and chocolate are her happy place, and she plans to live the rest of her life taking it as and how it comes, just one day at a time.

Claire Casapao

Claire Casapao is an ambitious student who plays chess, writes thrillers, and plays the piano in her spare time. She always strives to do better than she already has.

Dr. Shritama Das

"One can just buy/borrow/receive/ steal a book, but never choose one! The only possibility is, either they can write or be chosen by a book!" The author Dr Shritama Das, a dental surgeon-turned-hospital administrator lives by this statement. She has co-authored eight anthologies comprising of short stories and poetries respectively. Few of her works are internationally published and are available as narratives on Spotify. Shritama displays her crafted clouds showering stories and thoughts for the audience to enjoy in her personal blog on WordPress and on her Instagram respectively: - https://wordpress.com/view/shritama09.wordpress.com https://www.instagram.com/storyteller_shritama/

www.ingramcontent.com/pod-product-compliance
Lightning Source LLC
LaVergne TN
LVHW012104160826
845678LV00014B/2927
9789390882786